A Sea of Stars

Kate Maryon is officially addicted to writing!

She also loves going into schools for talks and writing workshops, and is always so touched by the many emails she gets from girls telling her how much they've enjoyed her books. Kate loves spending time with her grown-up children, her husband and all her lovely friends and continues to be inspired by the work she does with children and adults, which supports them in discovering the truth of who they really are. But wherever she is, whatever she's doing, there's always a story running through her imagination, the shadow of a character forming in her heart.

Kate still loves chocolate, films, eating out, reading, writing and lying on sunny beaches and she still dislikes peppermint and honey.

Also by Kate Maryon

Shine

Glitter

A Million Angels

A Sea of Stars

Kate Maryon x

HarperCollins *Children's Books*

First published in paperback in Great Britain by HarperCollins *Children's Books* 2012
HarperCollins *Children's Books* is a division of HarperCollins*Publishers* Ltd,
77–85 Fulham Palace Road, Hammersmith, London W6 8JB

The HarperCollins *Children's Books* website address is
www.harpercollins.co.uk

1

A Sea of Stars
Text copyright © Kate Maryon 2012

ISBN 978-0-00-746464-7

Printed and bound in England by
Clays Ltd, St Ives plc

Chapter 1

Sometimes I wish...

I've wanted a sister forever. Even before Alfie was born. Then after him I kept wishing and wishing and wishing but she never came along. So I'm going to remember this summer holiday forever, even when I'm an old lady with grey hair and wrinkly skin. It's hard to believe how much has happened between finishing school and starting back again tomorrow. It's as if these huge hands came down from the sky, picked up my life, tipped it upside down and shook it, like one of those beautiful snow dome things. And I just stood there in the middle while everything got all mixed up and blurry. But

then the snow started to settle and now I have to keep pinching my leg to remind myself it's actually true. Here I am, on the beach, alone, waiting to catch some zabaloosh gnarly waves, and my mum isn't even panicking. And I feel like squealing and jumping up and down because my sister, Cat, is actually clambering down the cliff to join me, with her surfboard under her arm. She's actually getting in the water. We're actually going surfing together. And you're never going to believe it but six weeks ago I hadn't even met her. I knew she existed but I'd only seen her face in photos and on the DVD, not properly in the flesh. I didn't know her beetle-black hair smelt like custard or how loud and ear-splitting her screams would be. I didn't know how much she'd nibble-nibble-nibble on her nails. I had no idea how frustrating and irritating she'd be (and she really is frustrating and irritating sometimes). And I couldn't have even imagined in my wildest dreams that the sight of her running across the sand towards me would make my heart unfurl like a huge pink flag to wrap her up in love.

Some people wish they had mystical powers so they could see into the future and know what's actually going to happen. Or that there was this big book in the library where your whole life had been written down. Dad says everything is planned. He says it's already mapped out in the stars and that we choose our life and our family and friends and everything that's going to happen to us way before we're even born, when we're just tiny twinkling stars in the sky. Some people think its God that has this great life plan drawn out for us, or Buddha or Krishna or Allah – someone like that. That it was their huge great hands coming down from the sky and shaking up my life.

I don't know if I believe any of that stuff. All I know is that, after everything that's happened, things still aren't perfect with Cat and me; having a sister is nothing like it was in my imagination and it probably never will be. But things are what they are. This is how it is now we're sisters.

Chapter 2

A million more damselflies whirred...

The first time I said the word 'adoption', it felt like I was drinking from one of Nana's special crystal glasses. Like the word was something really precious, something to be careful with. But that was a whole year ago, so now it's more like a toothbrush or a spoon. When Mum and Dad got married they planned for a really big family – you know, the ones that look like they're about to burst out at the seams. The ones that have a million pairs of trainers by the front door and mountains of food in the cupboards. But, after Alfie, they'd been too scared to try for any more. It was kind of weird because we

never really talked about it but the fact that I was an only child clung to the air like the saddest day in the world.

Then, a few weeks ago, Susannah, the social worker, phoned to say she'd finally found us this ten-year-old girl called Cat to adopt. Mum was so excited her knuckles turned white gripping the phone so hard. Dad's eyes spilled over with tears and he hugged us both so tight I could hardly breathe. And I should have been excited; I should, because who wouldn't be when their dream had just come true? And I tried really hard to smile about it, but I couldn't get my lips to work properly. I just froze to the spot and my tummy clenched up as if my insides had turned into this big skipping rope and someone was knotting it up all tight. A million damselflies started whirring and fluttering in my throat, making me feel wobbly, like I might fall over and be sick.

"You OK, sweetie?" asked Dad. "You look a bit pale."

I nodded. I picked up Peaches Paradise, my cat,

hid my face and buried a little tear in her fur. I didn't even know why I was crying. I just had this big crushing feeling in my heart, like someone had dropped a car on my chest.

A few days later, Susannah sent us a DVD of Cat that she'd made with Tania, her foster mum. Dad tipped popcorn into a bowl and Mum made us hot chocolate with marshmallows on top.

"Be careful, Maya," said Mum, handing me mine, "and sip it gently; it's still too hot to drink."

I wished she'd stop treating me like a baby. I slid closer to Dad, dipped my finger in the chocolaty froth and licked it. But I didn't say anything because I didn't want to spoil things. The sun was streaming through the windows, bouncing off the sea and it felt perfect, us all curled up on the sofa, together.

"She's much smaller than I imagined," I said, after a while. "I mean, I'm only two years older and I'm much, much taller than her."

Mum nodded and wiped away a tear. "Just look at her, though," she said. "She's so cute! So sweet! Look at those big eyes, that shiny black hair. I can't

wait to meet her."

Dad was spellbound. "I can't quite believe it." He smiled. "You know, after the whole adoption rigmarole and all those forms and red tape, a whole year later, here she is, at last – our new little girl!"

I gripped Dad's hand and held my breath while we watched Cat on the swing, Cat sipping juice, Cat with her blue-black hair shining like a beetle's wing. She was nibbling her nails and chatting to Tania about a big, fat snail that was slithering up the wall. She turned to us and waved. A teeny smile crept around her cherry red lips and I kept thinking, OMG, I can't believe this girl is going to be my sister. My sister. My sister!

When the DVD finished, I let out my breath and Dad and Mum and me stared off into the distance for a while without speaking. My brain started whizzing at a hundred miles an hour. Seeing Cat on the DVD made her much more real than talking to the social workers about her, or making her the book about our family. The words that tumbled out of Mum's mouth a year ago, when she'd read

the newspaper article about adoption in Cornwall, had actually turned into a real live girl.

That night, I lay awake for hours trying to imagine Cat sleeping in the room next to mine. I imagined us calling out goodnight to each other and sharing secrets and stories. I imagined us giggling and messing about until Mum got so cross she had to stomp up the stairs and shout. I wanted Mum to shout. I wanted her to be a normal Mum who wasn't treading on eggshells all the time, so afraid that something bad might happen to me. I giggled and imagined Cat and me brushing each other's hair a hundred times like they do in *The Railway Children*. I saw us doing drawing together and playing. I'd teach her how to surf and make cupcakes and paper cranes.

I really did want all those things and I really hoped my imagination might make me feel happy and excited. But, with every new thought, the skipping rope inside me pulled tighter and tighter and a million more damselflies whirred. I looked out of my bedroom window at the bay below.

The oily black sea was swishing the world to sleep and the lights from the village and the night sky reflected on the water, a twinkling sea of stars. I looked out and wondered about so many things. Then I yawned, snuggled down in my bed and pulled Peaches Paradise under my duvet. I held her close and whispered into her ear.

"Is it true what Dad says? Did I really choose Cat when I was just a tiny star? Did Cat choose me?"

And now it really, really is happening. There are no more days left to wonder because Mum and Dad have gone to meet Cat. I wasn't allowed to go, so I'm with my best friend, Anna. Susannah said it was better this way, but I think that's stupid. This is my family, but now I feel left out and pushed away and my tummy won't stop whirring. I can't tell Anna because, although we're besties and we tell each other most things, she doesn't understand about whirring tummies and worries. Anna likes to be happy, happy, happy. Her mum's made us fish-finger sandwiches – our favourite – and we're

dipping them in ketchup and watching *Dr Who*. Anna's goggling away and hasn't even noticed that I'm not really watching; she can't feel that my insides are all tugging and twisting.

Later on, when we're busy making cupcakes for pudding, Anna looks at me. "Adopting Cat must be really weird. I've been thinking about it," she says, "and wondering… aren't you scared your mum and dad might like her more than they like you?"

A huge cold pebble grows in my throat and tears start stinging my eyes. I make a few big blinks to get rid of them and swallow hard. I keep stirring and stirring the cake mixture round and round and round. I've been worrying that Cat might not like me and that I might not like her. But I haven't even thought about Mum and Dad liking her best.

"Do your mum and dad like your sister best then?" I say.

"Well," says Anna, pulling herself up on the worktop and licking cake mix from the spoon, "they say they like us both the same, but anyone can tell it's not true. Evie's so little and cute, everyone loves

her – they can't help it."

When we've finished decorating the cakes and have eaten three each with hot chocolate, we go into Anna's bedroom to make paper cranes.

"I s'pose it might've been the same if Alfie was still here," she says, "they might've liked him best too. Everyone always loves the baby of the family. It's a fact."

My eyes go all misty. I can't see what I'm doing any more and I wish Anna would just stop talking. I've never felt like my mum and dad didn't love me. My mum's so panicked about me all the time I sometimes feel like she loves me too much. But maybe Anna's right; maybe that's why they've always wanted another child. I mean, I'm quite pretty, although my hair's a bit wispy and wild, and I'm nearly top of my class at school, but maybe... I try and fold my paper crane into shape, but it goes all wonky. I scrunch it up and feel lonely inside, as if my whirring tummy has opened into this huge dark empty cave. I stuff another cupcake in my mouth to fill the big scary hole.

"I think they like Alfie best already," I blurt out, spraying vanilla cake crumbs everywhere. "I know they love me and the social workers wouldn't let them adopt if they thought there was a problem. But I can tell they never stop thinking about him. Alfie is always perfect in their eyes. Because he's dead, he can never do anything wrong, and I'm doing wrong stuff all the time."

"I think they should get rid of that shelf thing," Anna says. "My mum thinks it's a bit spooky to have all those pictures of him."

"It's just for remembering," I say.

But Anna will never understand about things like remembering because her life has been simple and straightforward and normal, not all complicated like mine.

The first five years of my life were brilliant until the Alfie stuff happened. Then a big red bus nearly killed me when I was seven and, ever since, nothing's been the same. My mum stresses about me being safe and well all the time and hates letting me out of her sight. I secretly think she's

worried I might die, but she's never actually said it in those exact words. She wouldn't even let me go on the Year Six residential week. She worried that my canoe might sink or the abseiling rope might snap. She was convinced the coach driver would fall asleep while he was driving and crash. It was really embarrassing. I had to make up some story about not being able to miss my nana's seventieth birthday party. I couldn't tell Anna because she'd just laugh. And I felt really stupid because I had to sit in with the Year Fives and do all my lessons with them for the week.

Mum really, really panics about me going surfing and she's tried to stop me a million times, but Nana and Pops and Dad are on my side. She's convinced I'll come to some tragic end in the waves. She'd like me to sit quietly and read books or make mermaids with her or pots with Dad. And I try to understand because the Alfie stuff and the big red bus must've been really hard for her. But sometimes I think she doesn't get that it's been hard for me too.

When we've finished tea, Anna and I rush to

the bay. My mum hates it when we go alone, but Anna's mum trusts us. Anyway, Anna's little sister, Evie, has an earache so her mum has to stay home with her. I feel a bit nervous, like my mum's big eyes are somehow watching from way above me in the sky, like she can see that we're alone.

Surfing is my best thing ever and today the sea is amazing. It's so sparkling and clear that we can see little fish darting under our boards like silver streaks of lightning. It's hard to explain what surfing really feels like, but close your eyes and just imagine that the rest of the world has disappeared. Imagine that nothing else exists or matters except you with your arms stretched wide, flying on top of a tumbling, unstoppable wave. An amazing white horse, with froth fizzing around your feet and the salt on your lips and the sun melting your face into bliss. Imagine surfing through blue, blue sky, through fluffy white clouds with the wind in your hair, to heaven and far beyond. Imagine being the wildest and freest girl alive, then times that feeling by a trillion and you might start to get what I mean.

Dad says I must have salt water in my veins because I love the sea so much. The truth is, surfing's the only time I feel free.

Anna and I surf until our arms and legs ache so much they almost drop off. Then we play mermaids. We swish around in the waves and clap and sing, "A sailor went to sea, sea, sea, to see what he could see, see, see, but all that he could see, see, see, was the bottom of the deep blue sea, sea, sea," about a thousand times. Then Luca paddles up and starts splashing us like crazy.

"Are you gonna enter the surf competition at the end of the holidays, Luca?" I ask, when the splashing has stopped.

"Dunno," he says. "Dad won't say when we're going back to California. I like it here; it's totally cool." He smiles, his eyes bright sapphires in the sun. "Paddle battle?"

So we have this amazing paddle battle and then Anna and I gang up on Luca and we splash and splash until he holds his hands up in surrender. It's funny to think that Gus from the Surf Shack

Café is Luca's actual uncle, especially when they sound so different. Luca's Californian accent makes Anna and me laugh so much I'm scared my sides will split or I'll pee my wetsuit and turn the entire sea yellow. And for a while I forget all about Cat and the adoption and Mum finding out we're alone because everything fades away.

Then I spot Mum and Dad clambering down the cliff, waving their arms like mad.

"She's perfect, Maya!" shouts Mum, smiling and racing towards me. "Absolutely perfect! You're going to love her, I know it!"

"And she's so excited to meet you, sweetheart," says Dad, folding me into a big papa-bear hug. "We've got great plans for tomorrow!"

"You must be so excited!" squeals Mum, dancing on the sand.

I nod and tug my lips up into a smile, but I don't truly feel it inside. My head starts clanging with worries, my tummy starts whirring and churning again and the rope twists tight. Mum goes on and on about Cat so much she doesn't notice Anna

and I are alone; she doesn't even notice I've been surfing without a grown-up watching. You'd think I'd be pleased about it, but somehow it feels like she doesn't care. And deep, deep down at the bottom of my heart, I wish Mum had never found the article on adoption. I wish we could change our minds.

Chapter 3

It's a massive step for me too...

"Huuurrrrrry up, Mayyyyya!" sings Mum, like an opera singer the next morning. "We don't want to be late for Caaaaat."

I don't remember Mum ever being this cheerful. It's as if someone has filled her up with flowers and sunshine and light and they're bursting out of her. I'm hurrying as fast as I can, which isn't very fast because the damselflies have multiplied since breakfast. They're whirring and fluttering so much it's impossible to calm down.

I can't decide what to wear. I've tried ten things on already, but nothing looks right and my hair's

gone stupid too. Every time I try to brush it straight it flies everywhere like it has an entire life of its own. I wish it was as shiny as Cat's, or hung down all chunky like hers. I wish it was a better colour, either black or blonde or red, not just wispy rabbit brown.

Mum's been going on all morning. She keeps saying Cat this and Cat that and I wish she'd just shut up. The thought of meeting Cat is making my palms feel sticky. It's different from when we went to pick up Peaches Paradise. She was just a tiny kitten and that was exciting; I was over the moon. And it's different from starting school or learning to surf for the first time on my own. It's different from anything I've ever done before. Eventually I have to give up worrying about clothes because Mum keeps on telling me it's time to go. So I throw on my new jeans, a white top and my flowery Converse. I look OK, but I'm so nervous my fingers keep slipping on my laces. I'm scared I'm going to sick my breakfast all over the floor.

Dad's already waiting in the car. He starts

honking the horn like crazy. He's singing along, really loudly, to some old Bob Dylan song on the radio and he's so smiley, if you were passing our house you'd think he was about to go on holiday for a year.

My insides are juddering.

"Remember, Maya," says Mum, when we're doing up our seat belts, "we mustn't overwhelm Cat with too much information. She's nervous and a bit shy, which means we need to give her lots of time and space. This is a big day for her, having all of us together – a massive step. We need to be gentle."

"Let's keep it simple," says Dad, turning Bob Dylan down, "then build up slowly to when we bring her home in a few days time."

"I do know that!" I snap, feeling really annoyed. "You've told me a million times before, you don't have to keep saying it. I'm not stupid!"

My heart is blazing and the damselflies are whirring sick burps up to my throat. I swallow hard to push them down and wish my mum and dad wouldn't talk to me like I was a stupid five-year-old.

I wanted to feel happy today. I wanted to be excited about getting a sister and now it's all gone wrong. I turn the little parcel I got her in my hands. It's wrapped up in silver paper with pink ribbons. It's hard choosing a present for someone you've never met before and I'm scared Cat won't like it. I glare at Mum and kick the back of her car seat – not hard, but hard enough for her to glare back at me and sigh.

"Maya, sweetheart," she says, "this is supposed to be an exciting day. Let's not spoil it with bad tempers."

She looks at her watch then tells Dad to pull over at the Surf Shack Café.

"We've got plenty of time," she says. "Let's stop for a quick coffee so we can all calm down."

I'd like to tell Mum that I'm only all calmed up because she's treating me like I'm five! I know this is a big deal for Cat, but it's a big deal for me too. My mum should know that, she's read enough leaflets on adoption and she's been to enough meetings and support groups. She's even got all these friends on

Facebook who've adopted children too. And I've got no one. All my worries just buzz around my brain searching for somewhere to rest. I've never met my new sister before, either!

Dad pulls over and parks next to a pale blue and white VW campervan with a stack of surfboards piled on top. I wish I could just grab one from the roof and go surfing. I leave the present in the car and follow Mum and Dad into the Surf Shack Café. When they see us, Rachel and Gus, the owners, give us a huge round of applause. Then everyone else joins in and we're the centre of attention, which makes the sick in my throat start to burn.

"Big day today, huh?" says Gus. "I think it's a totally awesome thing you guys are doing."

"It just feels right," says Mum, smiling and finding my hand. "Let's hope we do well by Cat. It's lovely that she'll have so many people from the village welcoming her too."

Then Gus looks at me.

"How's it for you, Maya?" he says. "You must be so excited to have a sister at last."

I nod and fake a smile, but I pull my hand away from Mum's. Gus makes me a hot chocolate with whippy cream and coffees for Mum and Dad. Rachel hands us three big slices of coffee-and-walnut cake.

"On the house," she says, "Celebration time!"

The Surf Shack is hot and steamy and filled with sunshine. Everyone's crushed together on long wooden tables, and laughter and chatter spiral up to the ceiling with the smell of coffee and cake and cheesy garlic bread. Dad grabs some high stools and we huddle together at the bar. I sip my chocolate and try to nibble at my slice of cake because it's my favourite, but it sits in my throat like a stone. I can't get the idea of Mum and Dad liking Cat more than me out of my brain. It keeps whirring around and around and I know it's stupid and it's spoiling things, but I can't help it.

I go to the bathroom and splash my face with cold water. I go really close to the mirror and stare. I trace my finger over my reflection, around my hazel eyes and my lips and nose. I look horrible

today. My face is all tight and twitchy and pale. I'm supposed to look happy; I'm supposed to be excited. But what if Cat doesn't like me? What if Mum and Dad do like her more? What happens to me then? I practise making a cheerful face. I take a big deep breath, fold up all my worries and tuck them deep inside my heart.

"Can we hold hands?" says Mum, when I'm back from the bathroom. "Just for a moment?"

"Muuuuuum," I say, checking no one's looking at me. "I'll look like a total dork!"

"You won't look like a dork," says Dad. "You only ever look gorgeous. Listen to your mum, Maya; this is important."

I know it's important. This is the last time it's going to be just the three of us. It's going to be so different being four. So weird. And a part of me wishes I could just turn the clocks back. Maybe if I tried hard enough I could turn them right back to Alfie and find a way to keep him alive.

We hold hands and I try really, really hard to

block everything else out. I try to push away the sick burning in my throat, and the stupid thoughts and the whirring damselflies and tight skipping-rope knot in my tummy. I try to focus. I cross my toes and hope that Anna and Luca or Izzy and Scarlett won't walk in, because they'll think I'm a total freak if they see me like this – and a freak is much, much worse than a dork.

"I just want to say thank you," Mum says, looking at me and then at Dad. "You know… for being my family. For loving me even when I'm all anxious and panicked. For being patient when I'm shut up in my studio making mermaid sculptures for hours."

Dad doesn't say anything, but a lump the size of a frog keeps bobbing up and down in his throat. He gazes at us one at a time and gently squeezes our hands. Then his voice croaks open. "I love you, my special girls."

Tears well up in my eyes and I can't help it. I forget about Anna and Luca and looking like a dork and I forget about all the crazy thoughts

spinning through my brain because I know deep down that none of that really matters. I know that my mum and dad love me.

"Thank you too," I say. My voice goes squeaky and fat silver tears spill over and leave snail trails on my cheeks. A huge wave of love pulls through me. "You're the bestest parents in the world, even though you worry about me way too much. I love you. And I'm glad that when I was a tiny star I chose you to be my mum and dad."

Mum's cheeks flush pink and Dad can't stop smiling through his tears. And I want to smile and cry too because I mean what I say. But there's this earthquake rumbling beneath me, this empty place growing bigger inside.

"Dad," I say, "do you think adopted children pick out their birth family and their new family when they're just tiny stars in the sky? Do you think they know deep down what's going to happen to them?" And I can't help adding, "Do you think Alfie knew he was going to die?"

"I'd like to believe that's the case, sweetheart,"

he says, "but no one really knows, not absolutely for sure."

We drift like clouds into our own private thoughts and I stare at my slab of coffee-and-walnut cake. I hope Dad is right. Because then somehow dying or getting adopted wouldn't seem so bad. Somehow, whatever's going to happen to me wouldn't worry me so much because it was all meant to be.

I just wish someone would tell me if it actually is true or not, or that I could zoom up to the stars and ask them, or up to heaven and ask Alfie.

Chapter 4

Same as me, Daaaaad...

We drive into the city and when we arrive at Cat's foster home, 14 Navy Way, my legs turn to jelly. Dad knocks at the door and a kind-looking lady with a very big bottom, soft green eyes and three little kids clinging to her legs appears.

"Hello," she smiles. She looks at me. "I'm Tania and you must be Maya. Lovely to meet you." She bustles us all down the sunny hallway. "Come on, come on in."

Then we get to this other door. It's painted white and has little black chip marks and sticky grey fingerprints all over it. Tania stops at the door then

looks at me and smiles.

"Ready?" she says.

My tummy starts flipping and twisting and knotting because I know that Cat is on the other side of the door. I cling to Mum's hand. My knees are virtually knocking against each other and I wish Alfie were here too. Tania opens the door and a girl on the sofa with beetle-black hair and cherry red lips half stands up then sits back down. She makes a little wave at Mum and Dad and then starts twiddling her fingers, keeping her eyes stuck fast to the floor.

"Here she is," says Tania. "Come in and say hello."

We shuffle in and sit down. My heart is drumming in my ears so loud all the other sounds disappear.

"Hello, Cat," says Mum. "This is Maya." Her eyes start brimming over with tears. "And, Maya, this is Cat."

Cat flicks her eyes up to me then sticks them back on the carpet, like the pattern is suddenly

the most interesting thing in the world. She keeps twiddling and twiddling. Mum sits down next to her on the faded green sofa and gently shuffles a little bit closer.

"Hi," mumbles Cat.

"Hi," I say, my voice cracking open.

And then my legs wobble and I stare at the carpet too. I'm feeling so dizzy that the pattern starts swirling around, making me feel sick again. I don't know what to do. I should say something friendly or serious because this is a really serious moment in my life. This is my sister. My sister!

I've waited for her forever and here she is in front of me and I'm just standing here like a dummy. I take a breath and try to say something, but my mouth's gone dry and my tongue keeps sticking to my teeth. The words in my head start fluttering around like snow in a snow-dome, whirling in the wind and I can't sweep them up together to make any sense. They keep bundling and sticking in my throat like damp litter. I'd like to hold on to Mum's hand, or Dad's, but I'm frozen to the spot. I'm

scared, if I move, the coffee-and-walnut cake will come back up and make big mess on Tania's carpet.

Meeting your new sister for the first time isn't something you can prepare yourself for. It's not something you can read about in a book or have a lesson on at school. I thought today would feel really special, like when people bring a new baby home from the hospital, bundled up in a blanket.

Tania coughs. "How about some tea?" she says.

Cat glares at her.

"There's no reason to wait around," she says. "I've been in this dump long enough."

Tania sighs and wipes a smile across her face. Then the silence looms again and all we can hear are breathing noises and Mum dabbing a tissue at her stupid quiet tears of joy.

"OK," says Tania. "Yes, well…"

Then Dad coughs too and I wonder if we've all caught some kind of cough infection.

"Come on, girls," he says. "Let's go and get some lunch."

Back in the car we head out of the city towards

the pizza place on the beach. Pizza is Cat's favourite, but she doesn't look excited or anything, she's just lolling her head on the window and staring off into space. She's clutching on to a big book that says, 'My Life Story Book', on the front. She keeps twisting it around in her arms as if it's a baby she's trying to settle down. I wish I could peep inside and find out more about Cat's life. I twiddle her present in my hands and roll her name silently around my mouth. It chinks on my teeth like silver. Cat, Cat, Cat. My sister, Cat. My sister. Cat. I dare myself to say it out loud. I really want to.

My sister, Cat.

I want to touch her beetle-black hair because it's the shiniest I've seen and smells vanillery, like custard, not flowery like mine. I want to know what she's thinking about because I'm scared she's thinking about us, about Mum and Dad and me, and if she likes us or not. If I could see her eyes properly I might be able to tell, but she's too busy staring out the window. I wonder what it's like for her being in the car with us. What it's like moving

to somewhere totally new, to a place where you don't know anyone.

What is it like being with strangers who are your new family, who are taking you to live in their house where you don't know stuff, like where the Sellotape lives or what they have for breakfast? What is it like packing up your bag and leaving your old life behind?

"What's it like?" I whisper.

I didn't mean to say it. The words just popped out before I could stop them.

Cat glares at me. Her dark eyes burn holes in my skin.

"What's what like?"

"Nothing," I say, biting my lip. "It doesn't matter; I was just being stupid. It was nothing."

But Cat won't let it go.

"What's what like?" she says through gritted teeth.

A balloon-sized lump swells up in my throat.

"You know," I say, swishing my hand through the air, "all this! Meeting us and everything."

Cat turns her back on me; she stares out of the window and nibbles on a nail.

"What's it like for you?" she asks, still facing the window. "Do you even want me?"

Mum turns and glares at me. I scuff my foot on the back of her seat. Her words of warning ring loud in my head.

Don't overwhelm her, keep it simple.

My mouth goes all dry again.

"I want you," I say, "but it feels a bit weird. Um… it's really hard to explain."

"Dunno neither then," she says, lolling her head against the window and staring out at the trees.

I don't remember much about Alfie. I remember the doctor shaking his head and all Mum's friends coming over with candles and crystals and special remedies to try and make him better. I wandered about in the middle of them wearing my sparkly stripy tights, waving my magic wand, trying to help. But I wasn't very good at magic and he died. And I don't even have a wand now, but sometimes I wish I did.

I turn my back on Cat and stare out of the window thinking about the photo of me when I was a toddler, wrapped up in a sling. We were trekking in the mountains in Nepal and I was riding high on Mum's back with a big dribbly grin on my face. Dad was writing a magazine article called 'The A-Z Of Travelling With Toddlers' and we all looked really happy. We didn't need anyone except us. But that was before the worry of keeping me safe started eating huge chunks out of Mum's heart and carving deep lines in her face. That was before she disappeared into her misty haze of fear.

When we knew about Cat coming to live with us, Susannah told us to make this special book about our family to send to her. I'd wanted to put that trekking photo in so Cat could see that we used to have adventures. But Mum said we needed to put in photos of what we're like now, of our house and Peaches Paradise and Nana and Pops and normal stuff like that. She thought the mountains in Nepal would confuse Cat. I thought they might give her hope.

Mum swivels round in her seat again, her bright rabbit eyes squinting.

"It's so lovely to have you both together at last," she cries. "We've been so excited about today, Cat. And nervous – we're a bit nervous too. And that's normal. It's OK. It's a big day for us all."

Cat looks up.

"I've been thinking," she says. "Do I have to call you 'Mum'?"

Mum coughs, like Tania, with the hint of a song.

"I really don't mind, sweetheart," says Mum. "Whatever you feel comfortable with."

But I know that's a lie, I know Mum does mind, because her hand flies up to her cheek as if it's been slapped.

"What would you like to call me?" she says.

"Dunno," says Cat. "Not 'Mum', though. I've got one of them already and I know you're gonna be my new mum and everything, but…" her eyes slide over to Dad. Her hand touches his shoulder. "I wanna call you 'Dad', though," she whispers. "I've never had one of them."

I see Dad smiling in the rear-view mirror and a tiny — almost-like-you'd-not-even-notice-it, it's so teeny — dagger tugs and twists in my heart.

"You could just call her 'Jane'," I say, sitting up straight, "because that's her name. Or something like 'Mama-bear' or 'Marmalade', or 'Marjums', or even 'Mama-Jane'."

Cat looks at me like I'm five or something, like I'm a bit of dog poo on the bottom of her shoe. My cheeks burn. I'm so stupid. So pathetic. So babyish. This isn't fair! I'm supposed to be the big sister! I don't understand how Mum and Dad thought she was so perfect for our family. She's not cute or sweet at all. I stuff her present under Mum's seat, shrivel up inside and stare out the window so Cat can't see my eyes. They've gone blurry and stingy with fat salty tears and I hate it.

"Maya, why don't you give Cat the present you bought for her?" says Dad.

I can feel Cat sliding in her seat so she's facing me again. Then, when I look at her, her eyes are big and soft like a puppy's and her cherry lips are

fixed in a smile. I don't want to give her the stupid present now.

"That's a lovely idea," says Mum, smiling and swivelling round to face us both. She claps her hands together. "It's a lovely, lovely idea! Go on, Maya, give it to her."

I don't have any choice now; I have to give it to her. I wish they'd just leave me alone. You're supposed to want to give a gift to someone, not want to throw it out the window and hide. She'll probably think it's rubbish, anyway. It's all rumpled from being under Mum's seat and the ribbons are crushed. I turn it around in my hands. I'm too annoyed to actually give it to Cat so I just place it on the seat between us and slide it towards her.

"Is it really for me?" she says quietly, tucking her 'Life Story Book' in her bag and picking it up.

I nod and she rests it carefully on her lap, as if it's as precious as the crown jewels or something crazy, and stares at it and starts stroking it like it's a cat. And I can't be angry any more because the stars come out in her eyes and a stupid sad feeling starts

filling up in my throat again.

"Really, really?" she says, twiddling the crumpled ribbons.

"Really, really," I say. " I hope you like it. I spent ages choosing it."

Cat opens the present carefully. I usually just rip the paper off straight away, but she unties the ribbons and then gently pulls off the Sellotape without tearing the paper even one bit.

"It's… it's… beautiful," she says.

I'd wanted to buy Cat something special, something she could keep forever. And after looking round for hours I'd chosen a musical jewellery box from my favourite shop in town. It's silver and has hearts and flowers embossed on it, and the inside is this soft squishy nest of red crushed velvet. Cat opens the lid and gasps out loud as a little ballerina girl in a perfect white tutu springs up and twirls round and round to the tinkling music. But then she snaps the lid shut and starts nibbling her nails again. She flicks her eyes over to me, hugs the box close to her heart, and mumbles so quietly I almost

miss it: "It's the best thing ever."

At the pizza place, Cat sits next to me. She's a very confusing person. Mostly she's a thunderstorm, brewing and nibbling, but, when the stars come out in her eyes, she shines. I kind of do understand why she doesn't want to call my mum, 'Mum', but I think she said it in a bit of an evil way. I know I can be mean to Mum too sometimes, but somehow that's different. I know it's wrong and I shouldn't do it, but she can just be so annoying.

I wish I had the guts to say to Cat, "Actually, I'm not going to call you Cat, because I have one of those already and she's much nicer than you." But I swallow my words back down when I notice her bitten nails. They're all crusty and scabby with blood where she's nibbled and nibbled so hard.

Cat, Cat, Cat. Her name chinks on my teeth like silver, it sits on my tongue like a bomb.

The waitress puts some menus on the table and I'm just about to pick one up when a text pips through to my phone.

What's Cat like?

It's from Anna and I'm about to text back the word 'Confusing' when Cat leans over and tries to read the message.

"Texts are private," I say, gently budging her away with my elbow.

"It's rude to text at the table, Maya," says Mum. "You should know that. Especially with Cat here, so switch it off right now! OK?"

"It's not rude," I say, looking at Cat. "I mean, she's my sister. It's not like she's a guest or anything. Anna does texting in front of Evie."

Dad glares.

"Not at the table, Maya," he says. "Now, be a good girl and put it away."

"I don't care," says Cat, twiddling her hair round her finger. "It doesn't bother me."

"Well, it bothers me," says Mum, pulling my phone from my hand and slipping into her bag.

"Come on, my girls," says Dad, smiling. "What are you going to have? Go for anything you like; we're celebrating, remember?"

I pick up the menu and stare at it. All the words are swimming about and the damselflies are whirring again. A million silvery wings whirring in nervous spirals. It's weird because I've ordered food in a restaurant a thousand million times before, but never with my sister here, never with Cat's custardy hair wafting up my nose. And my hands won't stop shaking.

"Margarita for me, please, Dad," I say, trying to sound normal. "And some garlic bread and a chocolate milkshake."

"What about you, Cat?" says Dad. "What will you have?"

Cat's eyes slide over the menu. She shuffles in her seat. She nibbles on her nails.

"Am I allowed a whole one?" she asks. "All to myself?"

"Yes, Cat," Mum laughs. "Of course."

"Don't laugh at me," snaps Cat, turning into a shark. "I didn't know."

Mum zips her laugh away and turns redder than her hair. She coughs and the air between us tugs

tight.

"No," she says, "of course not. I'm sorry, Cat. What would you like, sweetheart?"

"Meat feast, two lots of cheesy bread and a Coke."

"Mmmmm, I think I'll have the meat feast too," says Dad, stretching back in his chair and rubbing his hands together. "And, go on, I'll push the boat out and have a Coke as well."

"Same as me, Daaaaaad," says Cat.

Her words creep under my skin. It's weirder than weird hearing her calling him 'Dad' already. It makes my whole body whir and my heart feel empty and small. I know I have to share him now, we've talked about it loads, but I didn't think it would feel like this. He's my dad.

Cat looks in Dad's eyes and smiles. She turns her head a little bit to one side like she's unexpectedly shy, then she nibble-nibble-nibbles on a nail. Dad smiles back and winks. And the little knife in my tummy twists and bites as a spark of love flies from Dad's eye to Cat's heart. I pinch the back of my

hand. I should have ordered Coke and a meat feast as well, then I would've been in Dad's team too.

The waitress comes over and puts a pot of felt-tip pens in the space between Cat and me. She smiles and gives us each a poster for colouring in, even though we're a bit too old for it.

"Someone's birthday, is it?" she asks, tying purple balloons on the back of our chairs. "I love birthdays."

We look up, trying to think of what to say.

"Well, no…" says Dad, hunting for words and sending another wink to Cat. "But it is a very special day for our family. A very, very special day indeed."

Colouring isn't my favourite thing in the world, but it's better than watching Dad and Cat together, and it's better than looking at Mum's anxious glares. I'm busy doing an OK job of colouring in a stupid girl on a pony, when Cat's custardy hair wafts up my nose again, the beetle-black gleam of it shimmering in the light. She's leaning right over to look.

"I'm rubbish at colouring in," I say, quickly covering the picture with my arm. "I'm rubbish

at arty things. I like surfing best and camping and outdoorsy things – adventuring and stuff."

"Let me see, though," she says.

I slide my arm away and feel my cheeks burn.

Cat sniggers.

"It's lovely, Maya," Mum lies, picking up my poster. "It's really beautiful!"

We look over at Cat's. She's only done the pony's face so far, but it's amazing. I never knew anyone could make such a brilliant picture with such rubbish felt-tip pens. The pony looks almost real, like its eyes are actually glinting in the sun. And I'm so amazed by Cat's neatness that my body stops whirring. She hasn't gone over the black line once and the colours are so smooth and even, not scratchy and bumpy like mine.

"That's absolutely brilliant, Cat," says Mum, tugging the picture round to get a better view. "How do you do it so neatly?"

"Dunno," says Cat. "It's easy."

"An artist in the making," smiles Dad, sending her another wink.

 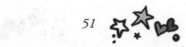

"Sshhhhh," she says holding her finger to her lips. "Stop interrupting."

She takes a deep lungful of air and holds her breath for ages while she colour-colour-colours. We stare transfixed at her concentration. I quietly scrunch up my page. I'm not an artist in the making. But if we were surfing I'd be better than her – or swimming, or making fires, or putting up tents.

This is the weirdest day of my life so far. Much weirder than when we started looking at adoption websites and all those faces loomed out at us, waiting for homes. Much weirder than Alfie dying or the time I was so excited about my new bodyboard that I kept it in bed with me all night.

When the waitress brings over our food the meat feasts look the best. They smell really yummy and the cheese is all gooey on top of big juicy chunks of salami and ham. Mum's salad is so colourful even that looks delicious, and suddenly my margarita seems boring and normal, flat and dull. I always have a margarita. Why didn't I have the meat feast as well? I'm really thirsty now too. The chocolate

milkshake is nice but it feels cluggy in my mouth and the Coke looks so refreshing.

Dad stands up and chinks his glass with a spoon. The forgotten rope in my tummy tugs tight.

"I'd like to raise a toast," he smiles. The lump starts wobbling in his throat again and Mum's eyes well up with tears. "To Cat and Maya and Mum and me; to all of us and our new life together. Cat, welcome to our family. We're a little bit crazy sometimes, and you'll have to forgive us for that, but we do have lots of fun and we're very excited to have you join us."

"Errr… thanks," Cat mumbles. Her face flushes red and her eyes dart around the restaurant, checking no one's looking. And with all the toasting and welcoming and eyes full of tears and throats full of lumps, Dad doesn't notice, and neither does Mum, that, quietly like the shadow of a robber on a dark, dark night, Cat slips a whole portion of cheesy bread into the bottom of her bag.

As we're leaving the restaurant, I slide up close to her.

I long to say to her, "Cat, I've waited my whole life for you to arrive. I've dreamt about us being together for years. And I know things feel a bit confusing right now, but they will get better – they have to. I have so many ideas for us, so many plans."

But the words get twisted up with my feelings and somehow come out all wrong, so what I whisper into her ear is, "I saw you."

Chapter 5

How precious it is, like a jewel...

The next day, we pick Cat up from foster care and go for a walk along the cliff path. I love walking the cliff path – it's my favourite, especially when it's windy and the breeze streams right through my hair. I'm charging ahead with my arms stretched out wide like a bird when Cat runs to catch up to me.

"You didn't say anything, did you?" she whispers. "About the garlic bread."

"I'm not a tell-tale, Cat," I say. "But you could've just asked. The waitress would have put it in a takeaway box and no one would've minded. You

didn't have to sneak it."

She blushes and nibbles on a nail.

"Don't go near the edge," she whispers, tugging my jacket. "It's too dangerous. You might fall."

"It's not dangerous!" I laugh, moving closer to the bit where the tufty grass ends and the ground slips away. "It's fun! I love it! Every time I go near the edge I feel like the sea is calling me down, daring me to jump off. It makes me so dizzy. Same with tall buildings like the Eiffel Tower and the Empire State Building. Come and stand next to me, Cat, and I'll show you. I'll hold you tight, I promise. I won't let you fall."

"No," she says, tugging me more. "I don't want to. Come back here."

I make my face go all ghosty. I wiggle my fingers in the air.

"Woooooooo," I whisper. "The mermaids are calling me down! Woooooooooo! Woooooooohoo ooooo!"

"Maya!" shrieks Mum, catching up with us. "Come away from the edge. If the wind caught hold

of you now you wouldn't stand a chance. You'd be down on the rocks in no time."

Dad laughs. He grabs me and tickles me and pretends to throw me down on the rocks so the fish and the mermaids can eat me up for tea. I start giggling for England and then Dad turns into the tickle monster and plays the game from when I was small. He tries to pull Cat in too, to get her giggling, but she and Mum back away looking scared, so it's just Dad and me shrieking with laughter and splitting our sides.

"Over you go," growls Dad in his tickle monster voice, holding me high in the air. "I'll feed you to the sharks."

"Stop it, you two! Please!" Mum shouts. "You're scaring me to death!"

Dad smiles and puts me down.

"Calm down, lovely," he says to Mum, folding her into a hug. "We're just playing."

I move even closer to the edge. We were only playing! We weren't doing anything wrong. We're allowed! I move closer and closer to the edge, so

close that if the wind gets a teeny bit stronger I might actually fall. Then Cat, Cat, Cat puts her hands over her eyes and starts screaming. It's a shrill, icy scream – a harsh, empty sound that rises up from a place deep inside her that's never felt sunshine. And, if you were watching, you'd think she'd seen a ghost. Or a silver-tipped dagger heading for her heart. Or a horror film labelled '18'. Anyone listening might think a murderer was kidnapping her.

We freeze for a second, shocked by the noise that's ripping up the sky. Then Dad and Mum rush to her side.

"It's OK, Cat," Mum says, fussing around. "We're here."

"You're safe," says Dad. "Maya's safe. It's OK."

Their words are like special cream to soothe her, but they don't help and Cat's scream goes on and on and on, slicing through me, shredding my ears.

"Cat," says Dad with a deep, firm voice, "stop this! Take a deep breath and look at me. You're OK. Maya's OK."

A lady with a dog walks past, her shoulders

hunched away from us, her brow knitted up with concern.

"That whole display was really unnecessary," hisses Mum, glaring at me and Dad. "Look at what the pair of you have done to her!"

"It's not my fault!" I shout. "We were just having fun. Me and Dad always do that! We always do the tickle monster."

"Not today," sighs Mum, pulling Cat in close, regardless of the continued screaming. "Not today. Remember, we're supposed to be taking things gently."

I feel angry now. Mum's fear and Cat's scream are like tight bandages on my legs, tying me down. Like great heavy boots on my feet. Cat's scream goes on and on, filling the sky, freezing the universe. Mum's face twists up with worry and panic. She strokes Cat's hair, she rubs her back, she mouths to Dad, "Oh, God! What shall we do?"

I hate Mum like this. I want my old mum back, the cool one from ages ago who let me crawl around in the mud and eat stuff off the floor. The one who

took me to festivals and climbed mountains in Nepal and slept on beaches in Italy, under blankets by the fire. Not this mum, who's trembling with panic.

Huge tears well up inside me, sharp knives cut the back of my eyes. My throat fills up with hard pebbles that are impossible to swallow down. I want the mum back who bathed me in a bucket and tucked me up to sleep in a drawer. I love her to the moon and everything, but if she had it her way she'd put me inside a silver bubble of light and surround me with a thousand golden angel bodyguards. I know she wants to keep me really, really safe so I don't die like Alfie, but she can't wrap me up in cotton wool forever. I have to be able to play with my own dad and have fun.

Dad looks from me to Mum to Cat; he runs his hand through his hair and sighs.

"Cat, sweetie," he says, kneeling down and clutching her shoulders, "listen to me. It's OK; we're all here. You're safe."

But Cat's scream just goes on and on and on.

She's hardly even stopping for air and everyone's staring at us like we're a bad family doing something wrong.

An old man walks past and mutters, "Disturbed, that one is."

Dad nods and stares out at the horizon, to the huge grey ship in the distance, travelling far, far away. I know he feels the same as me. Travelling was his whole life before Alfie and he wants that life back too. I know he does. Sometimes I see him exploring the world on Google Earth, having his own private mini-travel. But it's not the same on Google Earth – you can't smell the world from a computer or feel the wind in your hair.

My chest is burning now. I move so close to the edge that bits of earth start crumbling under my feet. I hold my arms out wide and let Cat's screams drill through my skin. I let the wild wind lick my face with its salty tongue. I stare at the jagged black rocks rising up from the sea.

"Get away from the edge!" shrieks Mum. "Maya, please! You're upsetting us all."

Then something in me snaps. I flash my eyes in defiance and start flapping my arms like mad, like I'm suddenly going to take off and fly to the end of the earth.

"Maya!" shouts Mum. "Will you do as you're told right now!"

Cat pulls her hands from her eyes. Her face is whiter than white. Her eyes are red raw and she just stands there, trembling. A part of me wants to run to her and tell her it's OK, but I was only playing; I wasn't doing anything wrong. Her scream gets quieter; it's all raspy and juddery, coming in great huge gulps. She stares out at the sea, like a deathly ghost is about to come and swallow her.

"Please, Maya," she says. "Please, I don't want you to get hurt."

"I'm not going to get hurt," I say. "I was just having fun with my dad! We were just messing about."

Cat stares into space. She starts nibbling on a nail and then a man attached to a paraglider runs past us. He jumps off the edge of the cliff, his kite

crackling and billowing in the wind. The ropes tug and pull at his chest as he flies through the air like a beautiful rainbow bird.

Cat stares at him and shudders. "I don't like your kind of fun. I hate it here." She turns to Dad. "Can we go now?"

"Yes, of course we can," says Dad, turning to leave. "Let's go."

I want to stay and watch the glider. I want to see where he lands. I want to stretch my arms wide with him and jump inside the clouds.

"We did that once, Mum," I whisper, kicking the ground, "when I was a baby. Remember? You strapped me on to you and we did paragliding in India. There's a photo of us in that box and the video."

Mum shudders.

"I was stupid and young then," she says, glancing back to watch the man. "I don't know what I was thinking. I could've killed you! I could've killed us both!"

"You weren't stupid, Mum," I say. "You were

brave. You loved exciting things! You loved adventure! And I didn't die, Mum. Look at me – I'm alive!"

Mum stares at the paraglider swooshing through the air. She shakes her head. She stretches out her arm, grabs me and pulls me away from the edge, back towards the car, scared my jacket might turn into wings and whoosh me far away.

I wish it would.

"Come on," says Dad, rubbing his hands together. "Let's go and get something to eat, shall we?"

Then, as sly as a fox, Cat's hand slips slowly into Dad's. I pull away from Mum's grasp and my hands hang empty and lonely, flapping about at my sides. And for the first time in my life I don't know what to do with them. They feel all big, like everyone can see I have nothing to hold on to. We're supposed to be having a nice time with Cat. We're supposed to be feeling all familyish and warm. But I'm as cold as winter, as empty as Alfie's cot. I don't mind Cat holding Dad's hand, not really. I know she has to.

I know she needs to because he's her Dad now too, not just mine. The problem is I'm sad I've never really thought about Dad's hand like this before, about how precious it is, like a jewel.

Chapter 6

I'm worried about everything...

We drive in silence for ages until Dad puts on the radio to fill up the car with sound.

"I'm sorry for scaring you," I whisper to Cat. "I didn't mean to; it's just Dad and me always play that game on the cliffs. We've played it forever."

Cat stares right through me like I'm not even there, nibbling and nibbling on a nail, twisting her hair round and round her finger and blinking her eyelids in the sun. I can't even tell if she's heard me.

"I am sorry," I whisper again.

I feel really bad now. This is a terrible day for me, but it must be a million times worse for Cat.

Dad pulls over and parks the car outside a thatched cottage with a swinging teapot sign above the front door. When Cat gets out of the car I notice her jeans are a bit too short for her and the laces on her trainers are bedraggled and frayed. If I were brave enough I'd take hold of her hand or touch her hair.

"They have gingerbread people living upstairs," says Mum, smiling and guiding Cat through the door, "and some of Father Christmas's elves are up there too, making all the cakes and goodies."

I know this is a lie, but, because Cat's ten and not twelve, her eyes start twinkling.

"Really?" she says.

Mum smiles and then Cat gets that she's being teased and slams her face shut like a book. She starts twisting her hair so fast and so tight that the end of her finger turns poppy red with blood.

"I didn't believe you anyway," she snaps, pulling away from Mum. "I'm not a baby, am I?"

"Oh, I'm so sorry, Cat, darling," Mum says. "I wasn't thinking. Maya believed that story for years.

Every time we used to come here, she'd sit wide-eyed, hoping to spot a gingerbread man or an elf. It was just a bit of fun. But I'm sorry, I won't do it again."

Cat's eyes burn black. She scrunches her face up in a frown. She looks from me to Mum and back again.

"Your family have a weird idea of what's fun," she scowls. "And stop saying 'sorry', both of you; it's boring, boring, boring. Nobody ever means it when they say 'sorry', anyway; they still go on doing horrid things."

Then she glares at Mum with fire in her eyes and snatches hold of Dad's hand.

The teashop is full to the brim with customers and crying babies. Ladies dressed up as Victorian maids in black pinafores, white aprons and mop caps bustle about with trays of steaming tea, happy smiles dancing on their lips. But we're not so happy. I feel lumpier and bumpier than before – worse than in the pizza place. I feel all quiet, all muffled, as if my mouth is full of cotton wool. And a guilty

feeling gnaws away at my bones as I glance at Cat's frayed cuffs. I wish I could take her shopping for some new clothes. I wish I could buy her some cool stuff. But the cliff walk and the sound of Cat, Cat, Cat's scream has turned our family into a delicate egg that might break into a million tiny little pieces, making me too scared to say anything.

Cat drums her fingers on the table. She tap-tap-taps her feet on the floor.

Dad sighs; he rubs his eyes and draws a smile across his face.

"How're you feeling now, Cat?" he soothes, putting more special word cream on Cat's sore life.

Cat twiddles with the sugar cubes. She pops one in her mouth and sucks. She keeps her eyes down low. "OK," she says.

"Because we'd understand if you didn't feel OK," says Mum. "What's happening in your life right now is huge and we want you to know that we're here for you, Cat. You're likely to feel really wobbly over the next few weeks, we all will, because of so much change. But what we do in our family when

we feel wobbly or worried about anything is talk. Share the problem and help each other through."

"We hope, in time," Dad says, "you'll feel safe enough to trust us with your worries, Cat."

She looks up. She tap-tap-taps her feet on the floor.

"I'm not worried."

I don't believe Cat because, if I were her, I would be trembling like jelly. But Cat freezes out every flicker of emotion on her face and keeps on tapping and tapping and twiddling the sugar tongs. She must be worried a bit, though. She doesn't even know us, not really, and in a few days time she's about to come and live with us, for good. Maybe she hides it all in her tummy or in a secret little box inside her heart. I wish Dad would soothe me with some nice words because I am worried.

I take ages deciding what to order. I really want the coffee-and-walnut cake, but Dad and Cat are having the scones and jam and cream thingy and I want to be the same as them.

I wonder what actually happened to yesterday's

cheesy bread that went back to the foster home in Cat's bag – if she scoffed it up all to herself or shared it around with the other kids. I wish she hadn't done it; it makes me feel a bit weird thinking my sister might be a stealer or something. There's so much I want to tell her: that the Sellotape lives in the left-hand drawer in the office; that we have cereal and yogurt and fruit for breakfast on week days and croissants and jam and bacon and stuff at the weekend; that we're allowed to read at night until 9pm and then we have to switch our lights off, but that I have a secret torch hidden under my bed. I want to tell her about Alfie and the shelf and everything. I want to whisper all my worries about Mum getting stressy and how scared she is about stuff since he died. I need to start talking to Cat about something, so eventually, when I've ordered the scones and cream thing, I get brave.

"I've got a ginger cat called Peaches Paradise," I say, "and she's really cheeky sometimes because she sneaks down to the harbour and begs for fish scraps when the boats come in."

"I know that," says Cat, twiddling and twiddling with her hair. "I saw all about her in that book you sent. The one with all the pictures."

It'd felt strange making the 'Our Family' book for Cat. I mean, how can anyone really tell what you're like from a bunch of pictures? It's the same as Dad's mini travels on Google Earth. Cat's DVD was much better; at least we got to hear her voice and watch the sunlight dance on her beetle-black hair. We just stuck pictures in the book. We had one of me surfing, one of me in the hammock reading and one of me in my uniform on my way to school.

Dad chose one of him making pots on the wheel, one of him in the gallery selling them and one of him out in the garden chopping logs. Mum chose the Sunday magazine photo of her that made her mermaid sculpture business so popular, one of her in the kitchen baking cakes and one of her last summer at the Surf Shack Café's barbecue.

I was worried about missing Alfie out. I thought he should be in the book because he is a part of

our family too – well, kind of. I suggested we took a picture of the shelf. Dad made it from gnarly old wood that smells of damp earth and moss and sea mist, and it has all Alfie's things on it: a photo of his tiny face, and the teeny-weeny plaster print of his foot, and feathers and blue eggshells and pink seashells and things that fly in on the breeze.

We could've written about how, every year on Alfie's birthday, we always have chocolate cake and a quiet little moment to remember him. How we always light the candle and Nana and Pops come over with a shrub for Alfie and a silver charm for me.

But Mum thought Alfie might be too confusing for Cat. She said there was plenty of time. So, instead, we put in photos of Nana and Pops in their garden and loads of pictures of Peaches Paradise. And some of our house too, and the beach, and Rachel and Gus, and people who hang out in the Surf Shack Café. We did doodles and sketches and filled the pages with glitter and tiny paper seashells and silver mermaids.

"Would you like a pet too, Cat?" says Dad. "Something of your own to take care of?"

And that starts up another worry. I'm not sure Peaches Paradise would like another pet in our house; she might get a bit worried and nervous too. But Cat's eyes shine and she draws a dog with her finger in a pile of salt she shook all over the table.

"Can I have a pony?" she asks. "Or an elephant?"

And Dad laughs and then Cat laughs too and a bright yellow butterfly of love with beautiful heart patterns on its wings flutters between them. They share a secret smile that makes my heart scrunch up small like a nut. And I'm really sad I've never sent him a bright yellow butterfly with hearts on its wings.

Later, when we've finished our tea, while Dad's paying the bill and Mum's looking through a tourist guide of fun family things to do, Cat walks right up to the cake display. She stares at it for a moment, licking her lips. My heart starts thudding hard against my ribs. She edges open her bag and twitches her eyes around the teashop to check no one is looking.

"You can't do that," I whisper. "You might get caught and then we'll all be in trouble. The social workers might stop the adoption or something. Dad'll buy it for you if you want it that much. You only have to ask."

Cat flashes her eyes at me, bright emerald green like Peaches Paradise's eyes when they sparkle and flash in the dark.

"I do what I want," she whispers. "No one tells me."

And, with the speed of a magician's hand, she quietly slips a huge slice of chocolate cake and a handful of sugar lumps straight into her bag.

Later, when we've dropped Cat off at Tania's and we're on our way back home, her words trample through my brain. I try them out on my lips, whispering quietly so Mum and Dad can't hear. "I do what I want. No one tells me." And they feel as shiny as gold as bright as the moon.

Chapter 7

I'm walking on eggshells...

The day after Cat's cliff-top scream, we decide we'll pick her up from foster care and bring her home for her first visit. Mum's stress is reaching an all-time high and the tension in the air makes me feels like I'm going to snap in half, as if my body is made of glass. Mum's really, really worried about getting things wrong with Cat – really, really worried I'm going to make her scream again.

"Please, Maya," she says, straightening the sofa cushions for the hundredth time, "keep things gentle. Just be easy and relaxed and normal, OK, sweetheart?"

I don't say anything, but Cat's words swim through my head. I do what I want. No one tells me. And they feel huge and powerful, like the Statue of Liberty on my tongue.

Then Mum starts stressing about the fact that she thinks Cat likes Dad more than she likes her.

"She needs to bond with me too," she says. "If this is going to work, she needs to bond with us all."

"Give her a chance," says Dad. "We've not even got her home yet. If you think about it, she's bound to find it easier to relate to me because she's never had a dad before. It's bound to be trickier settling to a new mum and a sister when you have a mum and a brother of your own. It'll take time for her to adjust."

Mum starts fiddling with her fringe and biting her top lip. I think she's jealous, like me. I think she saw the sparks and butterflies as well. I look down at the bay. It's a perfect day, the sun is shining and the waves look brilliant. I check my watch; if I hurry I've just about got enough time for a surf

session with Anna before we have to pick up Cat.

"Can I call Anna and meet her for a quick surf before we go?" I ask. "Her dad won't mind watching us; it's so clean and glassy out there – I can't miss it. Pleeeeaasssssssssse?"

Mum twitches. She checks her watch; she looks out the window.

"Oh, Maya, love," she says, "not now, eh? Not today. And, anyway, those clouds in the distance are brewing up a storm; it could get rough in no time."

"Please!" I say, "The clouds are miles away. It's perfect out there!"

Dad glares at me.

"Listen to your mum," he says. "You can't go down now, Maya. Maybe later, when we've got Cat."

"But I want to go surfing," I say. "It's no big deal; I won't be long."

Then Mum starts crying and Dad glares at me again, as if it's all my fault, so I shut up.

When we get to Tania's, Cat's wearing this strange red dress that's about three sizes too big for her, with long black socks and scuffed up school shoes. But her hair is still shiny; she still smells deliciously of custard; her lips are still like cherries. I decided on my new Roxy shorts and flowery top today, the ones that Dad and I bought in town. I can't wait to take Cat shopping, to see her in some normal stuff. I wonder what she'll choose.

"Can we go clothes shopping for Cat today?" I say, when we've picked her up and we're in the car.

"Maybe later," says Mum. "Let's go home for a bit first."

"I've got clothes," says Cat, stroking her weird dress. "I don't need to go shopping."

I open my window, stick my head out and sigh. Cat isn't easy to be around. She's awkward, like she's bumping into things all the time, like her thoughts are bumping into words. I watch the world zoom by, a very un-neat felt-tip pen scribble of grey and yellow and green. I wonder what happened to the chocolate cake Cat stole. Maybe it's still squished

up in the bottom of her bag or squashed under her pillow at Tania's. Maybe she ate it secretly herself or handed out little chunks to the babies.

Chocolate cake reminds me of Alfie. But lemon cake is worse because that's what we have on Alfie's dying day when we light the candle on the shelf again. Dad says the candle represents Alfie's spirit, lighting up the world. I like it and everything, but it's hard to get too sad about Alfie because I can't remember him — not really.

And it's weird because I can't really remember why we decided to adopt Cat in the first place, either. I remember Mum seeing the article in the paper and the little faces gnawing away at her heart. And I remember us agreeing that we have so much wonderful stuff in our lives to share. But after that everything seemed to happen so fast I don't remember actually saying yes.

I take a big, deep breath and the thick blue exhaust fumes rush up my nose. They punch my brain and make me feel fainty and sick. I quite like it. So I take another big, deep lungful, then push

my head out further so the cool fast air presses my cheek flesh to my bones.

I think maybe Nana and Pops were right. Because, when Mum first told them about us adopting Cat, they rushed straight over to our house.

"Do you think this adoption thing is wise?" I overheard Nana saying from the other room. "We're delighted to support you and we're looking forward to welcoming the girl in, but do you really have the time it takes to raise an adopted child? They're usually so troubled and they've been through so much. It's a delicate process, especially with older children. We're worried about Maya too; we don't want her to suffer."

They spoke like they were eating rhubarb without sugar, with their mouths puckered and pulled.

Mum's heart burned.

"They don't know what they're talking about," she said in her high-pitched squeaky voice when Nana and Pops had gone home. "Do they think we haven't planned to take time off when we get Cat,

to be cosy all together and settle in? Do they think the Adoption Agency would have offered us a child if they'd thought we wouldn't cope? My parents are ridiculous! We've had more education from the social workers and information support groups and books than we ever had when we were expecting Maya or Alfie. They don't put birth parents through the same rigmarole as this."

"Maybe they should," I remember Dad saying, "you know, test parents to make sure they're fit to take care of their kids properly."

"Don't lean out the window," says Cat, pulling on my arm. "It makes me nervous."

I stare at her. "Everything fun makes you nervous," I say.

She starts nibbling. "Doesn't," she says.

"Does."

Then she reaches into her bag, scoops a finger full of yesterday's chocolate cake and pops it in her mouth.

"Doesn't," she sneers.

"Listen to Cat," says Mum, twisting in her seat. "She's right, sweetie, it is dangerous. Get back in. There's a good girl."

I can't be bothered to argue. I shut the window and slump back down in my seat. It's like I have two mums nagging at me now, going on and on and on. Two scared people tying me down. I stare at the seagulls circling and swooping through the sky and wonder what my life would be like if I'd chosen to be a seagull or a beautiful yellow butterfly.

"I hope you like your room," I say to Cat, because I need to say something that will just go smoothly, like a normal friendly conversation, like normal sisters. "It's next to mine and looks right out over the bay. You can hear seagulls in the morning and see stars from your window at night. It's a really nice room. We've made it special for you."

Cat twitches and twiddles and blinks. She faces the window and starts nibble-nibble-nibbling on a nail. I'm walking on eggshells as my tummy ties itself up in knots. She doesn't answer me.

I think it's a game she plays, freezing people out,

making them feel clunky. A normal person would say, "Oh that's nice, I'm looking forward to seeing my new room," or "I love seagulls," or even, "I hate seagulls and wish they were all dead," but she doesn't say anything at all. It's really annoying; it makes me feel stupid.

Cat is just weird and that's a fact. I don't know if she's going to scream in my face or nibble-nibble-nibble, or stare right through me as if I don't exist. Susannah, the social worker, told Mum and Dad that Cat was really troubled inside and I need to remember that. She's been severely neglected and traumatised, so Susannah said her behaviour might sometimes be unpredictable. I thought unpredictable would be OK; I thought it might be fun, like she might play mad games and stuff. I didn't know it would be like this. It's like waiting for a dud firework to go off, wondering if it'll shoot up in the air and burst into colourful sparkles or explode and burn up your face. I want a sister, but deep down I kind of wish we could drop Cat back off at Tania's and pretend we never thought

of having her in the first place. It would have been better if Mum had read an article about travelling to Australia and got all excited about that instead.

Then I notice Cat's socks are all baggy and frayed around the top and that she has a great big scab on her knee. And my anger melts and I really, really want to hold her hand. The bedroom doesn't matter.

It's kind of strange that Nana and Pops buy shrubs for Alfie's birthday. Dad says it's symbolic; we can't watch Alfie grow as a boy, but we can see him grow through the shrub. When I was younger, I'd look at the shrubs for hours, trying to find Alfie's face. I sometimes wonder what he'd look like now as a seven-year-old boy. I wonder if he'd love surfing as much as me.

I don't know how to explain all this to Cat – how to tell her that every year, on Alfie's dying day, Mum spends most of the day meditating in silence while Dad and I snuggle down and watch films.

I mean how do you even start explaining your

family to a new person in a way they'll understand? It's like trying to unpick a spider's web or count each grain of sand on the beach.

It's not really the big things; it's more the little things. Like, we always have a star on our Christmas tree rather than a fairy because my dad loves stars. Like, Mum always has to let the phone ring three times before answering it – for no reason at all. Like, I always put the cap back on the toothpaste before I clean my teeth, whereas Dad does it after. The patterns our family makes are complicated and it's going to be too tricky to weave Cat in.

Chapter 8

Our house perches on a cliff...

Our house is perched on the cliff and, from a distance, is a grey-white seagull ready to open its wings and fly. Our garden is this amazing tangle of flowers. Dad's colourful pots are everywhere, bursting like crazy with blooms, and there are Alfie's shrubs and the big red hammock that's good for reading in. Mum's best silvery mermaid stretches across the lawn like a beautiful sea queen, shimmering and blinking in the sun.

"Look," I say, grabbing Cat's arm when we're out of the car. I try to pull her round to the side of the house.

She shrinks back, clutching her 'Life Story Book' thingy to her chest.

"Don't touch me!" she shouts.

We freeze and stare at one another. A little pulse starts throbbing in my cheek. Cat fixes her eyes on Alfie's shrub number two, a glossy-leafed rhododendron. She starts nibble-nibble-nibbling on her nail. Her eyes are glued to the ground.

"I'm sorry," I say. "I just… I'm so excited to have you home, I just wanted… to show you… this."

I point at the bright 'Welcome Home' banner that Dad and I strung across the porch this morning. It's flapping and fluttering and dancing in the breeze. Cat's eyes burn through the banner and I feel stupid and small again, like I'm five or something. And the banner looks stupid now too – really babyish. The letters are all wonky and the colouring in is all wrong – nowhere near as neat as Cat's. And it wasn't even my idea. It was Mum's.

"I don't like being touched by strangers," Cat says, nibbling and nibbling, "that's all. And stop saying 'sorry'."

I glare at her. My heart's on fire. Her words cut through me like broken glass.

"I'm not a stranger, Cat," I shout. "I'm your sister! And I'm trying really, really hard to welcome you and be friendly and nice, which is more than I can say for you!"

"I don't need a sister!" Cat shouts. "I've got a brother of my own, I've got my own real family. And I don't need you to be my friend. You don't mean it, anyway. No one ever does. You're just pretending."

Her eyes twitch around the garden. My mouth is dry.

"I don't even care about the stupid banner," I snap. "It doesn't even matter. I was just trying to be kind." I kick a stone across the patio. "I don't understand you," I say. "You're up and down and all over the place. You're really, really weird!"

"I know I am!" snaps Cat. "Everyone tells me, even my own mum! But I can't help it, can I? You don't know what it's like being me." She spins round and faces Mum. "Why don't you just call my social

worker now, before it's too late? Why don't you just send me back to Tania's? I don't care what happens to me and I don't care about you. Not any of you."

She looks at Dad, then she starts running. She bashes Alfie's shrub number five out of her way, leaving a trail of bright red petals, like big blobs of blood, on the path. Her legs move faster than the wind, through the gate, along the track, heading straight for the lane.

A storm brews across Mum's face. "I can't believe you just said that, Maya," she says. "We haven't even got her indoors yet."

And then we start running after her, calling, "Cat! Cat! Cat!" Her name chinks on our tongues like silver. "Cat! Cat! Cat! Come back!"

My cheeks are burning with shame. I didn't mean to call her weird. I didn't mean it! The words just popped out. I didn't mean to upset her.

"I'm sorry, Cat!" I shout, "I didn't mean it! I just…"

Cat turns to look at me, scalding my face with her sharp emerald eyes, her strange red dress flapping

in the wind.

"Can't you say anything else but 'sorry'?" she shouts, "It's boring, Maya. You're boring. Boring! Boring! Boring! All of you are. I don't even care what you think. I don't care about anything."

"Calm down, Cat," says Dad, "and come here! You can't just run off like that."

But Cat runs on and on and on.

"I do what I want!" she screams. "No one tells me."

She looks so little, her beetle-black hair straggly and tangly in the wind. She doesn't even know where she's running to; she doesn't even know where anything is. Fear flicks through my chest, a moth with razor sharp wings. I'm scared something bad will happen to her. I'm scared it'll be my fault. She might get run over by a car. She might run and run and run and get lost and then the adoption agency and the social workers will be really cross with me. It'll all be my fault! Cat'll probably tell everyone that she hates us and never wants to come back. Then they won't let us adopt again because

we're really bad people. And then Mum'll be so sad and she'll go to bed for a month, like she did after Alfie. She might even move us back to London and away from the sea.

I can't let Cat go. She has to like us. She has to want to stay.

"Cat!" I call. "Please! Please come back! I do want you! I chose you when I was just a tiny star; I've wanted you forever. Everything will be all right, I promise!"

I run harder than ever, my mixed-up feelings flapping around inside me like Mum's flip-flops, which are slapping the ground hard with fear of losing Cat, fear of her soft, sad heart breaking in two again. Mum catches me up and grabs hold of my hand. She clings on tight, as if we might fall off the planet if we slip. Tears are running down her cheeks and I'm sure she's not doing it on purpose, but her nails keep digging into my skin.

"I can't believe what you said to her, Maya!" she says, yanking my arm up and down. "She's traumatised enough already without you adding to it!"

I wriggle free from her clutch. I need to get to Cat.

"I'm sorry!" I say. Sharp silver tears pinch the back of my eyes. "I'm really, really sorry! I didn't mean it!"

I have to stop Cat running. I have to make her believe it will be OK.

Dad's eyes stay focused on the road.

"Cat!" he keeps calling, in a strong deep voice. "Cat, please stop this! We're not going to send you back. We want you! You're part of this family now!"

When we finally catch up with Cat, she's all snot and tears on her cheeks. She's standing on the grass verge by the edge of the big main road where the caravans and campervans come thundering down. She's rubbing her bloodshot eyes on her sleeve as if the summer hedgerows are making her itch. And she's standing there so sad and lost – more lonely than the last girl left on earth.

"You don't have to keep me," she cries, blinking her big emerald eyes. "I can go back, if you think I'm too weird."

93

"We don't want you to go back, Cat," I say. "I was just upset about the banner. I was trying to welcome you home and... I want you to stay. We all want you to stay. I won't touch you again without asking. I promise."

Cat crumples up like a sticky sweet wrapper. She clutches her 'Life Story Book' tight and sobs back her choking tears. A sharp stick jabs my throat, prodding me deeper and deeper into a huge dark puddle of shame. Mum opens her arms wide and I really wish they were for me because I need a hug so badly. I'm so shaky my teeth are clattering in my head. But Mum's arms are for Cat.

"I am sorry," I whisper. "I wish you'd believe me."

Cat sighs. She shrugs her shoulders as if she doesn't care about anything.

"Please don't keep saying 'sorry'," she sighs. "I've heard the word too many times before and it doesn't mean anything. No one really means 'sorry'. If they did, they wouldn't keep doing bad stuff."

I wish I could help Cat, but I don't know what's

happened to her. I don't know who's said 'sorry' and not meant it. I don't know what bad stuff they did. I start imagining her locked away in a dark cellar for years and years without any food. I imagine people hitting her and tearing at her hair. I imagine her feeling cold and lost and alone.

"Come on, poppet," says Mum, stretching out her hand to Cat. "Let's go home, shall we?"

Cat takes hold of Mum's hand and Dad stretches his out for mine. I grab it quicker than the wind. He squeezes it tight and love zooms up our arms and wraps up our hearts and ties bows around us like shiny birthday presents. All the tight knots inside me slip free and, although I've held my dad's hand more than a million times before, this time it's more precious than diamonds.

Later, when we're having juice together, Dad attempts another 'Welcome Home'.

"Welcome, Cat," he says. "Welcome, welcome, welcome to your new home. Please make yourself at home. Relax. Don't stand on parade."

Then he sits us all down and gets serious. He

puts on his lecture voice. I yawn. I can't concentrate properly on what he's saying because Cat's custardy hair smell keeps wafting up my nose. I wish I could reach out and touch it. But touching isn't allowed.

"The thing is," Dad says, looking at Cat, "we understand adopting you is very different from adopting a baby. You're a big girl and we totally respect you have another family. You're welcome to talk about them as much as you like. We're going to support you with the letterbox contact and meeting up with your mum and your brother, as planned. But we also want to make it clear that we're here to protect you, Cat. We're here to care for you and love you until you're a grown-up. It's our job to guide you, just like we guide Maya, so the world makes sense. And that means it's not OK to run off like that. It's not safe."

Cat stares through him with dull, empty eyes.

Then Mum joins in and Cat must feel like she's in the school office with the worst, most boring teachers in the world. She stares at the wall and nibble-nibble-nibbles on a nail; she licks away the

blood from a scab. Mum's words are grey-white seagulls circling round Cat's head, searching for somewhere to land. And I know Cat's not listening because of what she told me in the teashop. I know she's shut down her brain and is blocking Mum and Dad out. I do what I want. No one tells me.

I wish I could do what I wanted too. But I am a dog that's been very well trained and Cat is a fox running wild. I slide closer to Mum. Her mouth is opening and closing, as boring as the vicar at school, and she's saying stuff about it being our responsibility to keep Cat safe and out of danger.

I put my fingers up behind Mum's head to make bunny ears and, for a minuscule second, I manage to make Cat's eyes twinkle. And I can't quite believe it when she blinks the twinkle to me and it lands like a soft warm promise in my heart. Better than her colouring in. Better than if she'd liked the banner. Better than if I could stroke her hair. Like a golden rope of hope between us, with each of us holding an end.

"We know it'll take time for you to trust us, Cat,"

Mum's saying, "and adjust to all the new things around you, but we hope you will. We have your best interests at heart. When we met your mum, we assured her we'd care for you well. We know it's as hard for her as it is for you. It's hard for you both to be apart, and away from your brother. And we'll never try to take their place, Cat. See us, if you like, not as a replacement family, but as an extra one – extra love, extra support."

Cat slurps the last bit of juice, her teeth chink-chink-chink on her glass. She nibble-nibble-nibbles her nail. She casts her emerald eyes around the room.

"Can we stop now?" she says. "I'm bored. I don't want to talk about my family. They're private."

"Yes, yes, of course," says Dad, getting up and brushing invisible pottery dust from his jeans. "Sorry, Cat; we didn't mean to go on and on... We just... wanted... You know... Oh, dear, we're making a total hash of this," he says. "Look, Cat, welcome. Make yourself at home. Relax. Explore."

Chapter 9

My heart dips...

Cat travels slowly around the downstairs like a bus. She moves from place to place, stopping, waiting, looking, touching things, lifting them up to her nose to smell. I wonder if now's the right time to tell her about Alfie. I stand near to his shelf, hoping she'll be curious, but she just glares at me and passes without stopping to look. She tests out the big soft sofas instead, shuffling the colourful silk cushions until she's comfy.

"I like these" she says, hugging a bright pink cushion, "they're extra squishy."

I gaze down at the bay, at the glassy waves

glinting and shimmering in the sun, at the kooks making fools of themselves. I wish Cat would hurry up making herself at home so we can go down and surf. I'm sure she's going to love it when she gets in, especially when she sees the bodyboard and wetsuit we bought her as a surprise.

"Why don't we have a picnic on the beach?" I say.

"Good idea, Maya," Dad says. "Then you can have that surf you were hoping for this morning. The weather's still great. I'll sort the food while you and Mum give Cat the guided tour."

"We're up in the attic," I say, "you and me."

"Yes," she says, in a cold voice, "with the seagulls and the stars."

A tight band squeezes my heart. I try to catch her eye again, to catch the twinkle she blinked at me. But her eyes are flat and cold and dull. She stares straight through me, as if I were a ghost, as if I were Alfie.

We climb the white painted staircase to our rooms and my palms start sweating. Cat touches the

stripy lighthouse on the wall and pings the seagull hanging from a spring so it bounces through the air. She stops and looks at the thousands of photos of me, pressing her thumb on my two-year-old face, wiping bright pink birthday cake from my cheeky grin.

"I've never had a birthday cake of my own," she says, swallowing hard, "or a party. At Tania's I had to share my birthday with a baby. I made cakes for my brother, though. Once I made one out of a potato."

Mum squeezes my shoulder. She takes Cat's hand and a silver teardrop plops on her cheek. My tummy ties up in knots. I want to know more about what happened to Cat. Why did she never have a birthday cake? I start imagining the kind of cake Mum and I can make her on her birthday. It'll be the best cake ever. And she'll have this amazing birthday party with loads of friends and presents and her eyes will twinkle from the beginning to the end of the day.

We worked so hard to make Cat's room nice

for her, just like the banner. But I'm walking on eggshells now, scared she's going to hate it, scared she might start screaming again or run away. Mum swings the door open wide and ushers Cat in with a wave. Cat stops in the doorway. She peers around and sniffs the fresh smell of paint and brand new carpet. She takes a sharp breath in. I cross my fingers and hope to heaven and back, for Mum's sake at least, that she lalalalalurves what we've done.

The pale blue room floods with bright white light from the sea. Mum and I stand back while Cat busies herself around the room. She touches the white wooden bed, smells the pink and blue flowery patchwork quilt. She trails her fingers over the amazing yellow-and-white dolls' house Dad made for her that has tiny red roses painted around the door. She sits on the pink window-seat cushion and squints her eyes down at the bay. Her room looks like a perfect box of sugared almonds – so delicious you could almost stretch your arm out and eat it up.

And when Cat stands in front of our big surprise,

her eyes grow as round and bright as the sun. Right across one wall, Mum painted an underwater sea world full of beautiful mermaids and treasure chests and silvery fish and pink shells and magic. Cat strokes the wall with the palm of her hand. She peers at the glittery mermaid tails, trails her fingers along the seaweed. She smiles. She doesn't scream or stare through me or run away or freeze. And the tight knot inside me is just about slipping loose when she slaps us in the face with her words.

"I've been to places like this before," she snaps, nibbling her nail. "Some even better."

Down on the beach we try to smile and be friendly – even Cat's trying – but the truth is, everything feels clunky and sharp. Dad gets busy with the French bread and cheese and hard-boiled eggs, and Mum gets all fussy with the towels. She keeps straightening them, trying to make them neat and flat, but ends up getting sand everywhere. Dad makes his favourite cheesy joke about sandwiches, but nobody laughs.

I put my bikini on straight away because I'm itching to get into the sea. I need to practise my bottom turns and my pop-ups – especially my pop-ups – if I'm going to win the surf competition at the end of the summer holidays. Winning last year was easy because I had so much time to practise, but this year's different. And if Georgia Timson enters, she's so zabaloosh, I'll be dead for sure. Cat's staring at the bodyboard we gave her as if it were a monster about to eat her up. I give her some glitter wax and show her how to rub it in, even though bodyboards don't actually need it, and I work alongside her, rubbing some into my Minnie Mouse board as well. Talking about surfing is easy, so I start chatting away.

Cat loves the glitter wax. She does it really, really neatly, just like her colouring in. She gets so engrossed in it a little smile almost spreads across her face and I can't wait until we're in the water together. Maybe she'll blink me a twinkle again and I'll be able to catch it and blink one back. Maybe when it's just us, together in the water, being sisters,

it'll happen. I don't even mind if I don't get any proper surf practice in. Mum starts smiling, Dad starts whistling and it feels like everything's going to be OK. Mum holds up a new pink bikini and purple wetsuit for Cat to choose between and the damselflies start really whirring. But this time they're whirring with excitement instead of fear. I can't believe this is actually happening. I can't believe I'm about to go surfing with my sister.

"Which one would you like to wear, Cat?" asks Mum. "Bikini or wetsuit?"

Cat freezes. She shakes her head, zips her jacket right up to her neck and fiddles with the buckles on her shoes. My heart flips. The damselflies die and land in my tummy with a splat. Cat's face closes in; her eyelashes flutter.

"Come in with me, Cat," I say. "Please? I can teach you to surf. It's so zabaloosh! You'll love it. It's brilliant!"

Cat shudders, her face fades whiter than flour. She stares at the glittering sea and shakes her head backwards and forwards like she's shaking an evil

devil from her hair. Then her eyes grow dark, she drops her glitter wax on the sand and just sits there, staring and trembling, nibble-nibble-nibbling on her nails.

"I can't…" she whispers. "I…"

"Oh, come on!" I say, "Please?"

"Never mind if you can't swim, Cat," says Mum. "You could paddle until you're used to it. Or you could come for a wander and collect seashells and driftwood with me. It's just as much fun as surfing. We can make something out of them when we get back home."

But Cat shakes her head again, as if she were shaking bad, bad pennies from her mind.

"I'm happy here," she says, drawing a perfect heart in the sand with her finger. "I prefer just watching."

Then Luca runs up with his surfboard under his arm.

"Hi," he smiles. "Coming in?"

I'm not sure what to do, if I should stay with Cat or go with Luca.

"Go on in," says Mum. "Get some practise for the competition."

She slides really close to Cat.

"We'll watch you both from here."

I sprint to the water's edge with Luca; away from Mum and Dad and Cat; unravelling myself like sticky wool from the weirdness of everything; loving the pounding sound of my feet on the sand.

"Be careful," shouts Mum. "Don't go too far out!"

I throw myself into the waves and paddle out as far as I can go. Cat's words are sparkling on my lips. I do what I want. No one tells me. The surf breaks over my head and the waves drag under me, pulling me further and further out. And then I see my wave, swelling in the distance, coming closer and closer. When I catch it, I pop up on my board with my arms stretched wide like a bird.

On my tenth birthday, I thought that God or Buddha or Krishna or the Virgin Mary or someone truly holy must really exist. Because Nana and Pops

arrived with a bright red wetsuit and a real, real surfboard and some glitter wax for me.

I couldn't believe my eyes! My lips were lost for words.

I'd wanted a surfboard for ages, but Mum said there was no chance. Not ever. A bodyboard was one thing, but a real surfboard was stretching her patience just a little too far.

"I don't understand this obsession, Maya," she snapped, picking up the wetsuit. She glared at Nana and Pops. "And I'm really not happy about this! Surfing is a dangerous sport – really dangerous! You should have called me before spending a fortune on all this stuff; you should have asked me first."

Pops' eyes flamed.

"It's her passion!" he said. "Maya comes alive out there in the sea, anyone can see that, and I'm not going to stand back and watch you squash it. We supported you in everything you wanted when you were a child, Jane, and we'll support Maya too."

Dad said if I learned to do it properly then surely I'd be safe. He told Mum we couldn't move

to Cornwall and then ban me from the sea – that really wouldn't be fair. But Mum's worry spread over her like a rash, making her palms sweat and her voice go all shaky and her nerves jangle with fear. Dad won in the end, though. Mum didn't really have a choice, not with Nana and Pops and Dad on my side.

Surf school was amazing, completely zabaloosh, and the first time I stood up and surfed right to the beach without wiping out was totally the best day of my life. The glassy waves sparkled like magic and my heart swelled huge with pride. My surf coach smiled and clapped like mad.

"I'm totally stoked, Maya!" he said. "Girl, you rip!"

Dad was watching from the beach. He clapped and cheered and smiled and waved so much it got kind of embarrassing. He stuck his hand up in the air and stomped up and down on the sand, whistling like he was doing some kind of mad ritual tribal dance. Everyone stared at him as if he was totally bonkers. But, apart from Dad acting

like a total dork, I was the happiest girl alive. Now that I could surf properly and safely and I knew all the rules, Mum's fears would fade away. She'd get back to how she used to be and start bursting with exciting ideas. But then she scuttled across the beach with a picnic basket in her arms, and panic heavy in her eyes.

"I'm still not sure about this," she said, clutching my arm tight. "I know you're a strong swimmer, love, and a safe surfer now, and I do trust you, but I just don't trust those waves. Every time you're out there, I'm scared to death you'll get sucked out in a rip tide. I need you to promise me, Maya, that you'll never go surfing alone. Not ever! OK?"

Later, when Cat's back at foster care, Mum, Dad and I get talking.

"It's very unusual," says Mum, "for a ten-year-old not to love the beach."

"Probably can't swim very well," says Dad, making us a cup of tea. "Maybe no one got round to teaching her. Give her time; it'll work out."

He hunts in the cupboard for chocolate biscuits.

"Jane, love," he says to Mum, "any idea where those chocolate biscuits have gone?"

I know exactly where they've gone, but I don't squeak one tiny word.

"What's happening to Cat's little brother?" I say. "To Jordan? Can't we adopt him too?"

Mum runs her hands through her hair.

"No," she says, "The adoption agency did think about placing them together, but they decided against it. Cat's been like a mum to him for too long and it's not healthy. She still needs to be parented herself; it's not fair for her to feel responsible for a child. And Jordan – well, he needs to be parented by an adult, not Cat."

Dad takes hold of my hand.

"But we will keep them in contact," he says, "and the people adopting him are in agreement. She won't lose her brother like you had to, Maya, I promise."

Chapter 10

Dinner is quiet...

Mum, Dad and I have our last dinner together. Mum lays the table in the garden and picks pink roses from Alfie's shrub number three. She makes crème brûlée for pudding because it's one of my favourites and barbecued fish because it's Dad's top most favourite dinner. While we're waiting for the food, Dad's cleaning up the patio. He sweeps the dust and stacks the pots, then starts mowing the lawn, strimming the edges, and pulling up the weeds.

"There," he says, when he's finished, wiping a muddy hand across his brow and glugging down

a huge glass of juice without breathing. "That's better."

I don't think Cat will care what the garden looks like. I wouldn't even notice things like weeds and pots if I was about to be adopted and leave my little brother behind. But Dad feels it's right somehow to make the place nice for her. Mum says it's like when you're expecting a new baby and you start nesting and getting everything clean and ready. Then we imagine Cat like an enormous baby all wrapped up in a big pink blanket and us carrying her home in our arms. We start giggling at the idea of it and our giggles get so out of control we can't stop the tears streaming down our faces.

"Stop it!" says Mum, wiping her cheeks. "It's not funny!"

And for a moment a bit of the Mum I remember peeps through as her cheeks go all pink, her eyes shine bright.

I decide to start nesting too, like a big birdy sister. I run up to my room, pick up my dirty clothes and put them in the wash. I tidy my desk, make my bed

and even get the vacuum cleaner out to clean up the floor. Then I creep into Cat's room. It's still there, untouched. It's a peaceful holy place, like a church, waiting for Cat, like Cat's been waiting for us to be her new family. I rest my face on her pillow; it's smooth and cool on my cheek, her fluffy rug warm and soft under my toes. I sit on Cat's window seat and think about her 'Life Story Book'. I really, really want to see inside it. She knows everything about us from the 'Our Family' book we made, so it's not fair that I don't know as much about her. Mum and Dad have this huge folder all full of stuff about Cat, but I'm not allowed to look at that either because they say it wouldn't be helpful for my relationship with Cat. I wish they wouldn't treat me like a baby. I can know stuff, even bad stuff. I can cope. I am twelve! I look down at the bay and hope that soon Cat'll send me the golden twinkle again, that she'll show me her book, that she'll learn to like living with us. I hope one day I'll be able to touch her without asking, touch her hair without making her run.

Dinner is quiet. My cutlery feels heavy in my hands; it keeps clinking on my plate. The barbecue fish is tasty, but it's really dry and hard to swallow. I wish I wasn't so tame. I wish I were wilder, like Cat, more daring and dangerous. I take a sip of juice and start imagining what my life would be like if I could do exactly what I wanted with no one telling me.

Number one is I'd stop going to school straight away, except I might go and chat to Mr Firmstone sometimes. He's my favourite teacher because he tells us interesting stuff about life. When I told him we were going to adopt Cat, he told me that he was adopted too. He was found on some church steps when he was one day old, tucked up in a cardboard box. Number two is I'd move into a beach hut of my own, right down on the bay, so I could surf when I wanted without anyone saying 'no'. Number three is I'd eat coffee-and-walnut cake for breakfast with hot chocolate, marshmallows and cream.

"What happened to Cat?" I ask, when I stop thinking about my list. "Why did she get taken

away from her mum?"

Mum sighs.

"Sometimes, Maya," she says, "life just doesn't work out how we'd planned. When Cat's mum had her, she had wonderful intentions to be a good mum and do her best. But, sadly, her mum has the kind of problems that mean she can't care for her children properly. It's not safe for them to be with her."

"What kind of problems?" I ask. "Why wouldn't they be safe?"

"All sorts," says Mum, getting up and clearing the plates. "When we met her mum it was clear how sad and confused she is about losing her children. As much as she wants to look after them, she just can't. She's tried her best, but can't seem to get herself around committing to them and caring for them in the ways they need caring for."

"Deep down, Cat's mum loves her children very much," says Dad, "and we must always remind Cat of that. But sometimes it's hard for her to show them that love. It comes out all wrong and mixed

up and that can be scary for children. Children need stability, Maya. They need to feel safe and loved."

"How does it come out?" I say. "In what kind of way is it all mixed up? Did she get left on her own in the middle of nowhere or not fed? You know, like, did social services rush in with the police in the middle of the night and drag her away from her mum, screaming and scared, like they did on that 'Street Kid' programme I saw? Or was she at school, all quiet in the corner, with a teacher noticing that something terrible was wrong?"

"Cat will tell us in her own time," says Mum. "And there may be bits she'll never share with us or anyone else because it's just too painful. We need to give her time to feel safe."

"We need to help her feel safe and loved," says Dad. "That's the main thing."

It's late now – really late – and I should be sleeping. But it's hard to get to sleep knowing that tomorrow night Cat will actually be sleeping in the room next to mine. Making our house her home. Being my

sister at last. I look down at the bay beneath the cliffs, black and shimmering water under the moon. Peaches Paradise stretches and licks her paws. I tickle her tummy and she wriggles and purrs. I really want to know what happened to Cat and Jordan. I want to know exactly how life can get so mixed up that children get taken away. I mean, how can that actually happen? My life feels so boring and safe compared to Cat's that a part of me would like something exciting and dramatic to happen. I might feel different then. I might feel braver.

My imagination starts getting really carried away and I see Cat and me being those girls in the NSPCC adverts on telly. Like the ones where they're hiding, all scared and trembling in dark shadows, waiting for bad stuff to happen. And where boys in hoodies huddle together, hungry and dirty on the stairs. I imagine myself phoning up ChildLine to get help with some big problem that I can't solve on my own. I imagine the kind voice at the end of the phone making me cry. And I'm about to drift off to sleep with my imagination bubbling away

when Cat's words echo loud in my head. I do what I want. No one tells me.

That's when I send the text.

My phone trembles in my hands, my clammy fingers slip on the keys.

Really? texts Anna.

Really! I text back.

I creep downstairs. Mum and Dad are sleeping. I like being up so late, alone. It's like I'm in one of Dad's murder mystery films, with the house quiet and just the velvet silence of night-time ticking around me. I'm going to make an adventure of my own. All I need are firelighters, matches and a packet of marshmallows. I stuff everything into a bag, open the door and slide outside.

I really feel like I'm in a film now. I can't believe I'm actually doing this. The damselflies are whirring more than ever. Maya White doesn't do this kind of thing! The breeze ruffles through my hair. I shiver with excitement, loving the feel of adventure in my feet. I take a big deep breath, look up at the bright white moon and peel the layers of cotton

wool off me. I pop Mum's silver bubble with a pin and shoo the angel bodyguards away. I stand up tall and brave and alone, and a million twinkling stars rain down on me, tumbling through the night. The wind flaps sand in my eyes, my heart thumps loud in my chest and a voice yells loud in my head, Don't do this, Maya! Mum will go crazy if she finds out! But I don't listen. I don't care. I have to have an adventure of my own. Cat can't be the only one.

I start up the path and that's OK because the house is behind me, still warm on my back. I can still see my bedroom light and Peaches Paradise, stretching out on the window seat, watching me. Then I'm out on the track and a sliver of fear cuts through me, the damselflies whir in my head. A cloud travels over the moon and everything goes black. An owl screeches. A hedgehog scuttles past my feet. I should turn back, a part of me wants to. I almost call Anna to say, "Go back home this is a stupid idea!" But Cat wouldn't do that. Cat would do what she wanted, without anyone telling her what to do.

I open up the gate and it creaks like deathly white bones. I imagine skeleton hands reaching up from deep below the earth and dragging me down. I bury my hands in my pockets and turn my back to the wind. I keep walking further and further away from the house, my heart beating louder than a drum. I can do this. I can. I climb down the steep cliff steps; it's tricky in the dark and the stones are loose. I keep stumbling and tripping. I tear my jeans on a rock and graze my knee. It stings like mad. But I'm not going back now.

Down on the bay, the oily black water swishes and sways and shimmers. It looks kind of threatening and beautiful at the same time – a dark, shiny monster, stretching across the sand; a private, midnight lagoon inviting me to play. And the diamond stars studding the universe, and the twinkling lights from the houses, and the strings of little fairy lights along the bay twinkle in the water – a beautiful sea of stars.

And then I see Anna, already waiting.

"You're mad!" she whispers.

"Maybe," I say, "but I'm tired of being so good all the time. My life is so boring. I always do what I'm told. I need an adventure, and this is it. I've always wondered what it would be like down here at night, when everyone else is sleeping. Cat does what she wants and I'm two years older than her. I don't see why I can't too."

We gather up some driftwood, make a little fire and Anna clucks on about how crazy my mum will be if she ever finds out what we're doing. Then we giggle at our madness and squash marshmallows on to spindly bits of driftwood and toast them and let the sticky soft goo melt to warm sweet cream in our mouths.

"I'll race you!" I squeal, pulling off my jeans.

"Maya, we can't go in the sea!" hisses Anna. "It's too dark; no one's around. It's too dangerous!"

I glare at Anna. Her eyes cloud over with fear.

"I do what I want," I say. "No one tells me."

And Cat's words are gold and silver angels on my tongue. I turn away from Anna and race to the edge of the oily black water that stretches out in

front of me like a huge empty page. I don't care if she doesn't join me. That's her problem, not mine. I'm tired of people telling me what to do. I whisper so quietly that no one but the mermaids and the seashells and the fishes can hear, "I do what I want. No one tells me." And then I say it a little louder and, if I weren't so afraid of waking everyone up, I'd scream it at the top of my lungs.

Then Anna's right by me wearing nothing but her knickers and a wild tiger smile.

"Come on then, bumcake!" she whispers.

We charge into the sea, muffling our shrieks as the cold water freezes us and sparkles, all glittery on our skin. And we sing, "Bumcake! Bumcake! Bumcake!" like crazy and remember the day I sat on a bit of birthday cake at Anna's and no one noticed it for hours, until the squidgy blue icing had seeped right through my knickers to my bum. We lie on our backs, thread our hands together and float like driftwood on the waves. Everything's so black, if I close my eyes I'm not sure where I end and Anna begins, where she ends and I begin. We've been best

friends for so long and done so much together it's like we've actually melted into one person, with one brain and one warm heart, beating us into life. I hope it will be like this with Cat.

"Can I tell you a secret, bumcake?" says Anna.

"Go on then."

"Well…" she says, "you know Luca?"

"Errr… of course."

"Well…" she says, "I kind of like him!"

I start splashing her like mad.

"Luca?" I shriek so loud I have to shove my fist in my mouth so no one will hear. "Gus's nephew from California? Well, he is kind of cute, but you like him?"

And then I start giggling so much I think I might die.

Back on the beach, the shivers grab hold of us and chatter our teeth like hammers and nails. Our lips are like metal, like we've coloured them in with blue felt-tip pens or Halloween lipstick. I forgot to bring towels, so we prance about in front of our fire and pretend we're ballet dancers in *Romeo and Juliet*

and I can't stop laughing about Anna and Luca.

"Luca, Luca, wherefore art thou, Luca?" I giggle.

"Stop it!" laughs Anna. "I can't help it, can I? The other day he was just Gus's nephew splashing us and then the next time I saw him he made my insides go so mushy I couldn't even speak to him."

We hold our clothes near the flames to warm them and it reminds me of how my mum used to do this when I was small. Then we talk for hours and hours about boys and school and Alfie and Cat and new clothes and Luca and Anna. And we giggle and eat marshmallows until we're stuffed to the brim and our cheeks are aching.

When we're so tired our eyes feel hollow and the first pink wash of sunrise paints patterns in the sky, we let our fire die down. And when it's nothing more than crackling golden embers on the sand and thin blue smoke spiralling up to the sky, we say goodbye. We walk further and further away from each other, into the tie-dye silk dawn, and Anna gets smaller and smaller until she's just a tiny little zabaloosh speck in the distance and I'm just a tiny

bumcake.

"Zabaloosh!" she calls. "I love you the mooosh!"

Back at home, I feel scared. I stink of wood smoke and sea salt and lies. Guilt wriggles through me like a worm. If my mum has it her way, I'm going to be stuck to her and her fears until I'm at least a hundred. I pour myself some juice, find a biscuit for me, some fishy snibbles for Peaches Paradise and creep upstairs to my room. Even though I feel guilty, my body is tingling with excitement. I want to sing at the top of my voice or swing from the tallest tree and tell the world all about my adventure with Anna. I do what I want. No one tells me. But I can't risk Mum noticing the wood smoke smell, so I jump into the shower, dry myself off with a big warm towel and snuggle down deep in the warm patch Peaches Paradise made in my bed.

Chapter 11

She wouldn't stand a chance out there...

Cat's second icy scream comes after five days of her living with us and it shatters the dark night sky. I leap out of bed and race into her room. Mum and Dad thunder up the stairs and Cat's sitting up in bed with her eyes wide open, screaming and screaming at the wall.

"It's OK, Cat, sweetheart," says Mum, rushing to her side. "We're here; you're safe."

Mum wraps her arms around Cat to soothe her, but the shrill sound keeps coming and coming. I'm really worried about my eardrums splitting, about

Cat's throat breaking. I stand watching and the scream goes on and on and on. And it's worse than the one on the cliff because she's staring blankly and it makes me go cold inside.

"This is the night terrors Tania talked about," says Mum. "She said we shouldn't be afraid, Maya, because Cat's not aware of what's happening. She's lost in a bad memory, poor lamb."

"Thankfully, she won't remember any of this," says Dad. "Tania told us we mustn't wake her when it happens or talk about it in the morning. That'll just make things worse."

Cat starts thrashing about, trying to escape Mum's arms, screaming and screaming, as if someone is hurting her. Mum soothes and strokes her hair. Dad takes my hand and leads me downstairs to make some warm drinks for us. He takes one up to Mum and then snuggles on the sofa with me, while Cat's screams razor the silky smooth night to shreds. We try watching a movie, but it's impossible to concentrate, then Dad tries reading me a story, but focusing on that is even worse. So we end

up slumped and sleepy and snuggled, listening to music and playing cards. Just before 3am, Cat finally drifts off to sleep.

In the morning I feel like someone's stolen my body and put a huge heavy pumpkin in its place, like my eyes have been open since Christmas. I didn't feel this tired after my secret night on the beach with Anna. That day I felt lighter than a feather, like I was floating on air. I pull on some clothes and carefully, quietly, peep through Cat's bedroom door to see if she's awake. I expect to see her fast asleep in bed, or holding her breath and colouring in at her desk, but Cat's bed is empty. Her patchwork quilt is as straight and neat as her colouring in, and her puffy white pillows are stacked like a sandwich on the top.

Down on the next landing, Dad's still snoring. I creep into his and Mum's room and stand really close and watch them. Dad's lips puff out with his breath, Mum's mouth is droopy and little trails of dribble are spilling out. They look different when they're sleeping; it's as if someone's stolen my mum

and dad away and put waxwork models in their place. I shudder and go downstairs.

Everything's quiet and I go from room to room, looking for Cat. I check the kitchen and the sitting room, but they're empty. She's not playing in the den or watching TV or in Mum's studio or in the office or the bathroom or the spare room. I open the back door and creep outside. The sun's climbing higher in the sky and the garden path is warm under my feet. I shield my eyes from the bright light and watch the seagulls circle and swoop. I open my arms wide and stand on tiptoes and flap. I wish I could grow beautiful feathers and fly. When there are no places left to look for Cat, I start calling. Maybe she's hiding; maybe she's trying to have some fun.

"Caaaat," I whisper, careful not to wake Mum and Dad. "Cat, Cat, Cat," I say, loving the sound of her name on my tongue. "Are you hiding? Because, if you are, I can't find you and I'm too hungry to look any more. Let's go and get some breakfast and some juice. We could do some colouring in if you like. Or watch cartoons?"

Back inside, I listen for Cat's breathing. Maybe she's hiding in a corner somewhere, or behind the curtains. But all I can hear is the clock ticking and Peaches Paradise purring. Where are you Cat? I go round all the rooms again, hunting behind doors and under cushions, but she's not here. She's not anywhere and my heart starts bumping fast and I have this sick taste in my mouth because I know something must really be wrong.

"Caaat!" I call a bit louder, roaming backwards and forwards through the house. "Caaaat! Caaat! Caaaaaat! Come out now! This is getting silly. I've had enough of looking for you."

Dad tumbles downstairs, his hair all sticky-up and wild.

"What's all the fuss?" he yawns.

"She's missing!" I say, pulling on my sandals. "Cat's not here! She's gone!"

"Gone?" says Dad. "What do you mean, gone? She can't have. Where?"

He runs round the house, searching and calling, not quite believing what I've said. Mum tumbles

down, bleary-eyed too. And then we're like the emergency services, rushing about, all blue lights flashing. We run outside and call, "Cat! Cat! Caaaat!" Mum's slippers slap the ground like cold dead fish off the boats and we run down the path, along the track and out on to the road, calling. Through a line of caravans, queuing for Mr Egbert's campsite, past a trail of campervans with surfboards piled on top.

"I don't believe this is happening," says Mum, shakily. "Where ever has she gone?"

We race to the bay and into the Surf Shack Café.

"Has anyone seen, Cat?" Mum screeches. "She's disappeared; we've lost her!"

"Sorry," says Rachel, balancing plates full of breakfast. "I haven't noticed her, but we've been so busy this morning, she could easily have slipped through."

Then Dad notices the time.

"It's 11 o'clock!" he says. "I can't believe we slept so long."

"We were up half the night, remember?" I say.

Mum tugs on Dad's arm.

"Yes, but we should've got up," she wails. "I should've set the alarm. We should've been up for her. I can't believe I let this happen! What kind of mum am I?"

Panic writes across her face; memories of Alfie and lemon-cake days and big red screeching buses. Gus leaps into action. He calls the police and the lifeguard. Everyone in the café abandons their breakfast. They spill out on to the beach and wait for Gus to tell everyone what to do, which way to go, where to look. Then he turns to Luca and me.

"Look," he says, "someone needs to be home in case she comes back. "Luca, you take Maya back to the house and wait there in case Cat returns. Call my mobile if she does."

Our hearts pound faster than our feet as I show Luca the shortcut home. We scrabble up the cliff and I slip and cut my knee. But we keep on going, along the track, back to the path where our legs knock the roses. I turn back and look down at the

huge waves swirling and crashing below.

"She can't even swim," I say, my eyes blurry with tears. "She won't stand a chance out there."

Chapter 12

We hurt too...

When we get back home, I'm so out of breath my heart's exploding in my ears. We race through the door and something feels really weird. I'm expecting the house to be deathly quiet, like when we left, but the radio's blaring away and Peaches Paradise is lying on the window ledge, smiling, basking in the sun and licking her paws like she's just been fed.

"Cat!" I shout, rushing into the kitchen. "Are you here? Are you OK?"

Cat smiles. She's sitting on a high stool, jigging away to a tune while she's whisking eggs.

Luca phones Gus and tells him to stop the search party.

"Where on earth have you been, Cat?" I screech. "We've been looking for you everywhere! We've been really worried!"

"Where have you been?" says Cat. "I thought you were still in bed! And what's to worry about? I only went to get some eggs from the farm shop – no big deal! The lady was really nice; she gave me some sweets."

She sticks out a purple tongue to show me.

"No big deal?" I shriek. "Cat, it's a really big deal! You can't just wander off like that. I got up and you weren't here and we thought something had happened to you!"

"Something did happen," Cat says, in a singsong voice, too bright for someone who spent half the night up screaming. "I was hungry, Peaches Paradise was hungry and you were all sleeping, so I thought, Breakfast time! Then I tried to find some eggs, but we didn't have any, so I took some money from the tin and went to the farm shop to get some. Then I

gave Peaches Paradise some eggs and sugar and jam, which she really loved, and I thought I'd make us all some breakfast. As a surprise! My brother thinks my omelettes are the best, so I thought you might like them too!" Her sharp eyes glint like knives in the sun, her voice is as cold as ice. "Special treat!"

"Look," says Luca, "I'd better get back to the café. I'll leave you to it, OK?"

But I don't want him to go. I want him to stay and eat omelettes and pretend everything in our house is normal. I want to invite Anna over and then go down to the bay to surf.

"I'll be surfing later," Luca says. "You coming down?"

"Maybe," I sigh. "I'd like to, it's just…" I look at Cat, she's grating this big lump of cheese into a bowl. "I'll have to ask my mum."

Luca disappears. I turn back to Cat.

"Mum and Dad are going to go crazy at you," I say. "You're only ten years old, Cat – you can't just wander off."

Cat glares. "You might be my sister now, but

you're not the boss of me, Maya!" she says. "I've told you already. No one tells me what to do! No one! I've been going out on my own since I was five and I know what I'm doing, OK? I can go anywhere. Even in the city."

She pours oil into a frying pan, turns the hob on and stares at me with cold eyes that are all empty, like a room that's not been lived in for years.

"And you shouldn't be doing that either, Cat," I say, leaning over and switching off the hob. "Not without a grown-up here. You might burn yourself. Even I'm not allowed to fry stuff without a grown-up around."

Cat's eye's narrow until they're scary thin black strips of ice. I wish I could creep behind them and feel what it's like being her, all sharp edges and blackness and nibbles and screams.

She turns the hob back on and glares. "If I'd have waited for a grown-up to be around before I went shopping or made breakfast," she snaps, "I would've died ages ago. My brother would've died too!"

Cat's words slap me in the face. I don't want

anyone talking about dead brothers. It makes my skin sting.

"But you're not going to die now, are you?" I snap. "There's always enough food in our fridge; it's never been empty. Your brother probably has enough food where he lives as well. But that's not the point. You have to ask if you want to go out somewhere and you're not allowed to fry when no one's around. It's the rules."

Then Cat cracks, and pure egg-yellow poison runs out.

"I don't care about your rules," she spits. "I don't care about any of you. I've told you that before! All I care about is growing up quickly so I can get back to my brother and take care of him. And I don't even care about this…" she says, swiping her arm across the worktop. The whisked eggs and cheese and oil and tomato sauce tumble off the surface and smash on the kitchen floor. "I was just trying to surprise you!" she screams. "I was just trying to be kind! But I shouldn't have bothered; get your own breakfast."

Cat starts running again, splashing through the puddle of eggs and the smashed bowl, cutting her foot on the glass.

"Come back, Cat!" I say, sprinting after her. "You can't just run away all the time!"

She snarls and snaps. Her face is white with rage and reminds me of Mum's white knuckles on the day Susannah first told us about Cat. Mum races through the door with her bathrobe flapping. She opens her arms to catch Cat, but Cat dodges behind her and boofs straight into Dad. He catches her in his arms and swings her right up high, like he used to do to me when I was small.

"Hey," he says, "what's going on here?"

Cat thrashes and flails in his arms.

"Leave me alone!" she screams, punching him.

She sinks her teeth into his arm until it oozes little red dots of blood.

"Ouch!" says Dad, holding her tighter. His eyes narrow and burn right through her. "OK, young lady, that's enough!"

I've never heard Dad's voice so low before, so

calm. I wish I could do something to help him. I want to charge into her and bash her down to the ground and smash her to pieces like the eggs.

"Don't hurt my dad!" I scream, rushing to Dad's side.

Cat starts kicking me, she catches my tummy with her foot and it really, really hurts.

"And kicking," says Dad, tucking Cat's foot under his arm, "is not allowed! Not acceptable under any circumstances. Being angry is OK. But hurting other people is not!"

Mum pulls me into her arms. She holds me tight while Cat twists and spits like a deadly snake in Dad's arms.

"Let go of me!" she screams, pulling Dad's hair. "I hate you!"

Dad scoops her up higher and higher. Her fists bash against his chest. Her nails dig into his cheeks. Her screams slice the air and grate my skin like cheese. I hate her too. I don't care about her twinkle. My tummy's clenched so tight and I'm trying to blink back my tears, but they're

spilling over and over.

"If you calm down, Cat," Mum says, "we can talk about it. We're here to help you, sweetheart. Whatever happened, we can work it out, I promise."

"Get off," Cat barks at Dad. "Leave me alone!" She jabs Dad's ribs with her elbows, winding him, but he doesn't let her go, he holds on tight. "I said, get off me! Leave me alone!" she screeches. "I hate, hate, hate you! All of you!"

She's a wild tornado, whirling in my dad's big, bitten arms, in our dad's big, bitten arms. And then something rips open in my heart.

"You're not the only one who's had a bad time," I scream.

Cat stops thrashing. She holds her breath and stares right through me, as if she's not listening. But she is. I can tell.

"You're not the only one who's lost a brother and stuff," I say. "I had a brother once!"

One huge silver teardrop plops on to Cat's cheek. Her lip trembles. She nibbles her nail. Her face

crumples up and she buries it in Dad's shoulder, then cries and cries and cries. She shakes and sobs and wails and trembles for ages and ages and ages.

Chapter 13

Mum's gone all twitchy...

Since Cat kicked me, I've been really, really wary of her. I've never been kicked before. It's left this really big bruise that's turned all purple and yellowy. Cat's kind of folded up into herself, locked herself away so no one can get through. She's hardly speaking. She's doing lots of quiet, neat colouring in, holding her breath, resting the tip of her tongue on her lip. She keeps on staring into space, looking at nothing. Mum says she's probably looking at memories. I think she's trying to keep her brother's face in her mind, scared in case he slips away. Maybe she's replaying bad stuff that happened. Maybe her mind

is like one big, scary movie. I feel really creeped out by her because, behind her empty eyes, I can feel her brain ticking and ticking, watching us, thinking and thinking. I can hear it ticking in the night, when she's scuttling around in her room. She's put a note up on her door saying, NO ENTRI, PRIVIT.

Mum's gone all twitchy. She keeps fiddling with her lips. I overheard her talking to Dad the other night, saying she's worried about getting it wrong with Cat, saying she's afraid she's doing her more harm than good. I saw Dad stroke Mum's hand. He poured her a glass of wine.

"We'll get there," he said. "Give her time."

"Whatever's gone on for that child," Mum said, "the impact is devastating and I'm not sure I have it in me to turn her around. The adoption agency said it would be a challenge, but I'm not qualified for this. I thought lots of cuddles and good food and a loving family would be enough. But she won't even look at me."

A few days later, all these books on parenting adopted children and surviving trauma arrived in

the post. Mum hasn't put them down since. She keeps squealing when she's reading, getting excited with new ideas. When we were out shopping, she bought this little teddy with a red spotted ribbon round his neck. He sits in the middle of our table now and every day we have to sit down and say how we think he feels. Mostly, I think he feels bored just sitting there all the time, staring out at the world. I think he wishes he were a bird, so he could fly far away and have some fun. Today Mum thought he felt a bit sad and lost, like he needed a friend to talk to about his troubles. Dad thought the little teddy felt excited about something and was really ready to get on with it. This morning, when it was Cat's turn, her emerald eyes narrowed to thin, pond-green slits. She stared at the bear for ages and I was worried about what was coming next. I think Mum was too.

"I think he hates his life and he'd like to smash it up into little pieces," she said. "Then he'd like to run back to his cave and find his little tiny bear cub and give him a great big cuddle

and eat lots of chocolate."

Mum sighed. She fiddled with her lip. She made a cup of tea, handed everyone a few squares of chocolate and went back to her books. I wondered about what trauma actually feels like if you've got it, if it's an actual feeling under your skin or a thing in your brain or something else. I wish I could step into Cat's body for a minute.

Dad's not twitchy. He's got calmer. His voice is slower and lower. He's more patient and his eyes keep sending out beautiful butterflies to everyone. I wish I could catch one and tuck it in my pocket so I'll never forget how precious he is. Dad's started teaching Cat how to make pots because one of Mum's books says art can be good therapy. Cat won't talk to him, but she watches with beady eyes and then copies him and makes really, really good pots, as good as her colouring in. But if you say anything about them she just goes red. She stares straight through you, hides her face under her arm and nibble-nibble-nibbles on her nails.

Mum's going to try her on mermaids next

because she thinks Cat is a real artist in waiting. She wants to take her to an art exhibition at Falmouth University to get her inspired. I'm happy to go with them so long as Cat doesn't wear that stupid red dress and black socks. I wish she'd let us take her shopping and get some normal clothes. Sometimes she looks crazy, like yesterday when she wore this strange floppy hat thing and a brown knitted poncho. It was such a hot day I nearly melted in my shorts, but Cat shivered under her poncho like it was the middle of winter.

I wish Mum felt the same about surfing as she does about art. I wish she'd take me to Hawaii to get me inspired. I'm definitely going to be rubbish in the competition because I haven't done any training for days. Since our disaster picnic, Cat's refused to go down to the beach at all. And Anna's away camping, so I can't go down with her.

"Can I go surfing today?" I ask Mum. She's leaning over Cat, teaching her how to do a proper sketch of Peaches Paradise.

Mum peers out of the window at the perfect

glassy waves. She checks her watch. Looks at the tide tables. "I don't think so, love," she says. "Dad's out all day, so he can't take you down… Unless," she looks at Cat, "maybe we could all go?"

"Will you come, Cat? Please?" I say. "Just this once. You don't have to go in the sea or anything; you could just do drawing on the beach with Mum. We could have a picnic; it'll be fun!"

Cat's face goes white. Her hand grips her pencil and she starts scribbling deep grey lines through her work, making Peaches Paradise look like she's been struck by lightening.

"No!" she spits, jabbing the page like mad. "I just want to stay in and draw."

"Cat," Mum says, really gently, "we need to make sure Maya gets to do what she wants as well. You both need to learn to take turns. It's only fair."

Cat starts tapping her feet, almost kicking the floor, scribbling and scribbling over Peaches Paradise.

"I'm not going," she says. "You can't make me."

She takes this big deep breath in, presses her lips

together and sucks them back between her teeth. She stares at Mum and holds her breath until the room feels stretched so tight with waiting that Mum and I start gasping for air.

Cat keeps on holding and holding and holding.

"Stop that!" says Mum. "Come on, Cat, you're scaring me. Take a breath, sweetheart."

Cat's eyes start bulging. Her face glows red.

"I said, stop it, Cat!" says Mum, in a much sterner voice. She starts nibbling her lip. "Breathe! Now! Come on! There's a good girl."

I really want to breathe for Cat. My lungs feel squeezy and burny. I'm longing for a big gulp full of fresh cool air. But I'm kind of holding my breath too. So's Mum. We're stuck watching Cat, waiting and waiting and waiting.

"Cat," says Mum, carefully, "if you could tell us what's so bad about the beach, it would help. We might be able to help you through it. You never know, you might even enjoy it down there. We might have lots of fun. We could have an ice cream!"

Cat pushes her lips out. They're a purply-blue colour. Mum starts trembling. She looks at me. I look at her. I wish Dad were here because he'd know what to do. I try touching Cat, hoping it'll make her angry so she'll have to take a breath. But she just glares at me and shoots poison through her eyes.

"Stop it! Now!" says Mum, lightly shaking Cat's shoulders.

I don't know what to do. If I slap Cat she'll have to take a breath, but we're trying to teach her that hitting isn't allowed. And I'm just starting to panic when Cat suddenly starts shaking. It begins in her shoulders, they start trembling and trembling, then it moves down her body and, when the trembling hits her tummy, she takes this huge gasping breath and then bursts into tears. More and more sobs spill out of her mouth. Huge drops of silver roll down her cheeks. Mum gasps for air and starts sobbing too and I try to hold my tears back, but I can't. I'm so relieved Cat's breathing again and the tightness in the room has snapped that tears leak out of my

eyes too.

"Look at us!" says Mum, breaking into laughter. "Just look at us!"

Then we end up in a huddle, all crying together. Cat gets one half of Mum's lap and I get the other, but she still doesn't touch me.

"I just don't want to go to the beach," cries Cat, sitting up and blowing her nose. "Please don't make me!"

"It's OK," I lie. "I don't mind. We don't have to go."

Mum looks at her watch.

"No," she says, "its not fair, Maya. You need to have your turn too. And Cat, you need to learn that you can't manipulate people like that."

"I could go with Luca?" I say. "You don't have to come. He's probably out there, anyway. Maybe if we call Gus and Rachel they won't mind keeping an eye out."

Mum's face twists with concern. She looks at Cat.

"This isn't OK, Cat," she says. "If Maya goes

surfing with Luca, you and me need to have a serious talk. This breath-holding thing must never happen again!"

Mum phones Dad and the damselflies start whirring inside me. What if I am actually allowed out, alone? It would be so amazing, like Christmas and birthday and the best holiday anywhere in the world, all rolled into one. I cross my fingers behind my back and have to stop myself from holding my breath. Mum's umming and ahhing on the phone to Dad, shaking her head and nodding. Please, please, please, say yes. Cat's eyes are staring at nothing. Her pencil is digging and digging at the page, making deep grey slashes through Peaches Paradise.

I can't believe it! I'm actually going to down to surf without Mum or Dad watching, without Anna's mum or dad watching, without a real grown-up there at all. I'm allowed! I smile at Cat and silently thank her. If she hadn't held her breath, this might never have happened until I was twenty-five or thirty-nine years old or something.

"Please be careful, Maya," says Mum, nibbling her lip. "Don't do anything crazy. And I'd like you back in an hour. OK?"

An hour isn't really long enough. Not halfway long enough. But it's longer than I've ever had before.

"Please don't go," says Cat. She nibbles on a nail. "I don't like you in the water."

"You can't control me, Cat," I say. "You're not my mum. But I promise you I'll be careful. I always am."

I'm shaking like a leaf. Trekking down the cliff with my surfboard under my arm on my own feels really different. Different from when I went out that night with Anna because the secret guilty feeling of that is still burning a little hole inside me. Being allowed out alone is totally zabaloosh. I feel like a grown-up, totally wild and free.

Chapter 14

Big waves are the best...

When I'm down on the beach, I start searching for Luca. But there are so many kooks dorking about and kids with buckets and spades and girls in bikinis, swishing in the shallows, it's hard to see who's who. I really miss Anna. It's a bit weird being here on my own. It is exciting and everything but there's no one to get excited with. Being with Anna would be zabaloosh!

Eventually I spot Luca in the distance and paddle out to meet him. I sing, "A sailor went to sea, sea, sea, to see what he could see, see, see, but all that he could see, see, see, was the bottom of the deep blue

sea, sea, sea," but my voice isn't as loud as it would be with Anna. I feel a bit silly singing on my own. It is amazing, though, just being here. I paddle further and further out, the water shimmering under me like miles of rippling silk.

"Hey," Luca smiles, when I reach him, "out here at last!"

"Finally!" I say. "I really need to train if I'm going to stand a chance with the competition. D'you know how long you're in England for yet?"

"A while," Luca says. "My dad's obsessed with crop circles and stone circles and old Englishy things. He keeps dragging me off to marvel at stuff like it's the best thing on the earth."

"You should enter the competition," I say. "Although, if the Timsons enter this year, no one will stand a chance. They're this family I met at surf school and they're totally sick! Harry's pro, so he won't be entering, but Georgia, Kirra, Sonny and Robbie probably will. I'm going to go pro one day too, like Jamilah Star."

"Big wave surfer, then?" Luca smiles.

"Definitely," I say. "Big waves are the best. They're the really exciting ones because they're actually dangerous and everything else just fades away."

I smile and blush while I'm babbling on because I start thinking about Anna liking Luca.

"Well, I haven't actually caught that big a wave yet," I confess, "but one day I will! You wait and see!"

I really, really want to tell him about Anna liking him, but I know I can't. It's Anna's secret, not mine to tell, but it's eating me up. I want to know if he feels the same way about her. I want to find a way of getting them together.

Luca catches the next wave. It opens out like a dream and he rips. But then he takes a spill and Rachel from the Surf Shack paddles over to me laughing.

"Dufus! Luca! You rode that one like a kook!" I call out.

"Are you crushing on him, Maya?" Rachel teases.

"What?" I say, horrified. "No! I know someone

who is, though, but I'm not allowed to say."

Rachel laughs and lies back on her board.

"Sorry my mum called you," I say. "She thinks I'm gonna die out here or something. She's so paranoid! It's so embarrassing."

"Awwwww, chin up!" says Rachel. "I'm sure things'll settle down with Cat soon and then your mum'll relax again. Luca's always around and we're pretty much always here, so tell your mum not to worry. You're a strong surfer, Maya, but it's good to be careful. Hey," she says, pointing to the wave that's swelling on the horizon, "your wave!"

And then it's just me and the salt and the surf and the sun, and for a minute I truly am the wildest and freest girl alive. Then the wave closes in and I lose my focus and start wobbling and slipping and Luca waves his arms like mad from the shore.

"Wooooohooooo!" he whoops. "Big wave, surfer girl! Stoke me!"

Then he starts laughing and laughing and bending double with the giggles, so I shout out, "I can do this, you know! I'll beat you to Hawaii."

I totally wipe out. I'm hurled around and around in a washing machine. My leash is tugging at my ankle and the sand is stinging my skin. The whole world spins and spins until my lungs burn and all the air's squeezed from me and I almost burst open. When I finally come up for air I can hear my mum shouting. She's standing on the beach, panicking.

"What's the matter?" I say, running through the shallows towards her. "I was OK. I just wiped out – nothing serious."

"It's Cat again," she says. "She's gone and I wondered if you'd seen her. I wondered if she'd followed you down."

We check in the Surf Shack Café to make sure that Cat's not in there and then we climb back up the cliff. Mum's going on and on about how it's all her fault for not being a good enough mother.

"I just turned my back for a minute," she says, "to go to the bathroom, and then she was gone!"

"She'll come back," I say. "Don't worry so much."

But Mum can't stop worrying; it's swallowing her whole. After we've searched the house and garden

twice, and checked if Mr Egbert at the campsite or Matilda at the farm shop have seen her, and had three cups of tea in a row, Mum calls Dad on his mobile. But Dad's miles away – he's still in London, with his phone switched off, selling pots and things to this big, important department store. And, even if we could get hold of him and he left to come home straight away, he wouldn't be back till much later.

Mum paces up and down. She wrings her hands together. She sighs and calls her best friend, Dawne for advice. Then she starts panicking in case Cat's trying to call home and puts the phone down without even saying goodbye.

"Do you think I should call Tania?" she asks, "or Susannah or Cat's social worker?"

"Don't panic, Mum. She's used to going out on her own; she did it all the time when she lived with her mum. She'll be back soon, I promise you."

But Cat doesn't come back soon. We sit waiting for ages. Mum keeps trying Dad, but his phone is still switched off. I make us both a sandwich and

another cup of tea, but Mum just sits there staring at the sea, picking at the crusts, her teacup trembling in her hand. A fat silver teardrop plops on her cheek and I wish there was something I could do.

"If only she'd talk to us," says Mum, "we might be able to help. I should have made her come down to the beach. We should've all stayed together." She looks at me with firm eyes. "And I'm sorry, Maya, but I'm never letting you go down there alone again. Do you hear me? I'm never letting either of you out of my sight again."

Mum picks up the books on adoption and starts flicking through the pages, searching for a miracle or a magical key to unlock Cat. I blink and blink to fight back my tears.

"That's it!" she says, suddenly flinging the book on the side. "I can't wait any longer. I'm calling the police."

Mum's on the phone for so long, her knuckles turn white with clinging. I start whirring like mad, my arms and legs and everything all full to the brim with damselflies. Where is Cat? What is she doing?

Mum's voice goes all tight and trembly when she gives the police a description of Cat and the details about how she disappeared. I feel terrible. If I hadn't got Cat upset about asking her to go, none of this would've happened. It's all my fault. And what if something really bad happens to her? I keep looking out the window, hoping to see her beetle-black hair swishing. I look down at the bay. Cat wouldn't go down there, would she? She wouldn't have gone to watch me?

When the police arrive, Mum's trembling goes crazy. It's in her arms now as well – and her mouth, and her teeth. Her face keeps on twitching and I really wish my dad were here too. I make a pot of tea for the police and hunt for the biscuits, but someone has taken them. My hands are trembling so much, and I'm whirring and whirring, I slop the tea all over the floor. If only Dad would come home. If only Cat would come back.

Mum finds a photo of Cat. The police keep talking on their phones, describing Cat to the rest of the emergency services, whizzing the news of her

disappearance through Cornwall. The bus drivers and taxi drivers, and anyone else who might be able to help, now know that we're looking for Cat. I try Dad on his mobile again and leave yet another message and Mum calls Tania and Cat's social worker in case Cat's tried to make her way to them.

"I'm sorry," I say to Mum, miserably. "It's all my fault. If I hadn't asked to go surfing then none of this would've happened."

And what I want is for Mum to say, "Sweetie, it's not your fault. It's OK, she'll come back soon."

But instead, she rubs her eyes. She twists her fingers around each other, nibbles her lip then looks up at me. And, just like in a film, I can see Alfie's tiny face covered in lemon cake and the big red bus scribbling deep grey panic lines all over her. Like she's been struck by jagged lightning.

"I'm so scared, Maya," she says. "What if she doesn't come back? What if something terrible has happened?"

And I wish I could just crawl right out of my skin and hide.

Chapter 15

Errr, I stutter...

Mum and me are just about to say goodbye to the police when Cat suddenly skips up to the house — like nothing in the world is wrong.

"Cat!" cries Mum, running towards her, scooping her up into her arms and covering her with kisses. "Wherever have you been, sweetheart? We've been worried sick about you!"

"Talking about stuff is boring," says Cat, her green eyes shining like it's the most exciting day of her life. "You started to go on and on and I was bored, so I decided to go out instead."

Her eyes are full of twinkles, the most I've ever seen.

"But you can't just go out like that, sweetheart," says Mum. "We've told you before. It's dangerous; anything could've happened to you."

Cat shrugs and a huge smile spreads over her face. One of the police officers stoops down to her height and tells her she needs to listen to Mum and stay indoors and be safe like a good girl. Cat pokes her tongue out at him.

He pats her on the head. "Kids, eh?" He smiles.

Once we've said goodbye to the police, who reassured Mum that she was right in calling them, and that it's been their pleasure to help and no bother at all, a dark blue car pulls into the drive. Cat starts jumping up and down, hanging on to Mum's hand, jiggling it back and forth, over the moon with excitement. My heart is burning with rage. We've been so worried about her, so scared something bad had happened, and she doesn't even seem to care.

"I met a friend," Cat squeals, "and here she is! Isn't it exciting?"

A lady and a girl get out of the dark blue car.

"This is Chloe," she says, skipping, "and this is Chloe's mum!"

Then she starts gabbling on and on about Chloe's baby rabbits.

"Can I have one?" she says. "Dad said I could have a pet."

She starts squealing about how brilliant would it be if Chloe could stay for tea, how amazing it is that Chloe's going to be in her new class at school. I kick the ground and glare at her.

"You can't just keep running off," I say. "We were so worried about you. We called Dad. We called the police. We had the whole of Cornwall looking for you!"

Mum pulls Cat in close and stoops down to meet her eyes.

"Cat, sweetie," says Mum, "it all sounds really, really exciting and it's lovely to see you so happy, but I need you to know that running off like that just isn't OK. I need you to listen to me and understand. I was so worried about you."

"I'm fine!" says Cat. "Nothing bad happened."

Chloe's mum blushes pink, the same as Alfie's beautiful rose.

"Pleased to meet you," she says, stepping forward and holding out her hand for Mum to shake. "I'm Jules. I'm so sorry if we've created a problem."

Jules goes on and on about how she didn't even know Cat was with them. They've only just moved into the house up the lane and Jules was so busy unpacking things, Cat must've slipped in. She found her and Chloe in the garden, going bananas with excitement over the rabbits. And then Cat couldn't remember our phone number and Jules thought she should bring her back home. But then there was the worry about putting her in the car, what with 'stranger danger' and all that. So in the end Jules decided to drive along behind Cat, just to make sure she was safe.

I glare at Cat again. I could've had a proper surf if it hadn't been for her. It's not fair. Everything's always about Cat. If I'd just gone off like that, Mum would've gone crazy, stupid, mad. She'd have been all shouty and cross. Definitely not talking about

167

getting a baby rabbit!

Mum invites everyone in for a cup of tea and that's when I notice the metal things on Chloe's legs – like the dentist put braces on them instead of on her teeth. I know it's rude to keep looking, but I can't take my eyes off them. I want to know what they are. Cat doesn't even seem to notice; she's just jabbering on and on about rabbits and maybe getting one and choosing names and stuff. I'm wondering how Chloe can actually walk with the braces on her legs. I'm wondering how she'll get down the cliff and skip about in the sand. How she'll run. Or surf.

"Do you want to know about my legs?" Chloe asks.

Blood races to my cheeks and burns. I can't believe she noticed me looking.

"Errrr," I stutter, "I was just... you know... wondering how, erm..."

"You can ask as many questions as you like," she smiles. "Sometimes people talk to me in a baby voice like my legs stop me from hearing properly or

make me stupid or something. But they don't – not one bit!"

I keep my eyes on the floor. I nibble on a nail.

"I was just… I was just wondering how you'll manage the shortcut down the cliff," I say, "and running and stuff. What happened to you? Did you have an accident?"

Then, while the mums are chatting, Chloe tells me and Cat about her Cerebral Palsy, which she's had forever. It means her limbs don't work so well. She points to the brace things on her legs and tells us they're called splints. She tells us about the frame she uses for walking, and about her amazing neon orange wheelchair.

"The worst thing," she says, "is people thinking that because I have a disability I'm like I'm a three-headed alien from the planet Zog or something. Just because I get around in a different way, doesn't mean I'm any different from anyone else. The cliff might be hard, and the sand. But I'm used to things being hard and my family are really good at helping. We'll work out a way."

Cat slides so close to Chloe that their arms are actually touching. So close I know that Chloe will be able to smell her custardy hair. So close the little knife in my tummy twists and tugs and turns.

"Most of us have something to get used to," says Cat. Her eyes slide over me and silently stab my skin. "We're not all perfect!"

My insides start flapping about like a pigeon. My mouth goes really dry. I know I haven't had to pack my whole life up in a bag and go and live with a new family, or get used to my legs not working very well, but some stuff has been hard for me. I've had Alfie die. I've watched Mum being eaten up by fear.

"Some people's lives are just easy-peasy," Cat says, silently stabbing and stabbing. She snakes her arm around Chloe and whispers into her ear, "Some girls are just really, really spoilt."

"I'm not spoilt," I say. "I have hard stuff too. There's things you don't know about, Cat."

Cat pokes her tongue out at me and sends a twinkle to Chloe. I gather Peaches Paradise in my arms and run upstairs to my room. I need some

peace, some quiet time to think. I look down at the bay; Luca's still out there catching wave after wave after wave. It's not fair; I should still be surfing too! Peaches Paradise stretches out on my bed and purrs. She paws me until I stroke her tummy and she loves it so much that a little trail of dribble starts running down her chin. I don't want to cry. Not over Cat, anyway. But why doesn't she like me? Why will she let everyone else touch her but me? What have I done wrong?

Chapter 16

I glare at Cat...

Since Cat's disappearance over a week ago, we haven't tried getting her down on the beach even once.

"She needs to settle," says Mum, flicking through the pages of one of the trauma books. "We need to expose her to new things gently, take things slowly. We need to help her to feel relaxed."

And, even though the surf competition is only a few weeks away, I decide to be a kind big sister and teach Cat how to make paper cranes. We make hundreds of them together and I love the feeling of her next to me, nibbling and watching and carefully,

carefully, neatly, neatly folding the paper squares. Mum makes us chocolate brownies to munch on. Dad helps us string the colourful cranes on to these bits of wood and make a giant mobile, which we hang from the top landing ceiling. He fixes up this special spotlight so it shines on our mobile like it's a real piece of art in a gallery. I feel all warm and proud and special standing next to Cat watching our cranes fly about in the breeze.

Downstairs, Mum asks us how the little bear feels. I think he feels very proud of himself. Dad says he's feeling like an extra creative bear today. Mum says he's feeling very relieved and would like to sit in the sunshine with a nice cup of tea for an hour. When it's Cat's turn I hold my breath. Mum fiddles with her hair; she nibbles her lip. Dad taps his foot.

"I think the little bear feels more like a big bear today," she smiles. "He's maybe even a little bit taller."

Mum claps, she's so excited and Dad smiles. Then Cat and me set to work on this brilliant silver

and gold mermaid. Mum shows us how to cut all the soft metal stuff into little fins. We have to make holes in them and fix them all on to the tail so they jingle and shimmer in the light. While we're working, we listen to a Jacqueline Wilson story CD together and everything feels perfect. I don't even mind that it's non-stop sunshine outside and I'm stuck indoors. Because, suddenly, having Cat as a sister feels so perfect, just like in my imagination, just like we're living in a Disney film or something. And I even think Cat is enjoying herself too because she's smiling and sitting closer and closer to me. Then, just as we're finishing laying our beautiful mermaid on the lawn next to Mum's and standing back to admire it, Cat turns into a snake.

"Can I go to Chloe's now?" she says, firing her sharp little dagger tongue at me. "She's much more fun to play with than you, Maya."

I storm into the kitchen and pour myself some juice. I blink back the stupid tears that are swimming in my eyes. I don't care what she thinks of me! I don't! I just wish Anna would come back

from camping, then at least I'd have somewhere fun to go too. Cat skips in behind me and stares at the little teddy. Mum and Dad tumble in behind us; he scratches away at his beard, she hugs one of the trauma books.

"The little bear wishes he didn't have to live on this stupid table any more," Cat says, picking him up and stuffing him in her pocket. "He wishes he could go and live with Chloe!"

That night, when Cat's tucked up in bed, Mum, Dad and I have this big long talk.

"You've been amazing with Cat over the past few days," says Mum. "Really patient and kind. But we've been thinking… it's not really fair that you have to miss out on things because of her. And, as much as it worries me – you going out on your own, we think you're old enough to have a bit more freedom, more responsibility."

After what Mum said the other day about me never surfing alone again and never being allowed out of her sight, I can't believe my ears. I hold my

breath while they're talking, in case I break the magic spell.

"We've decided," says Dad, "that so long as Luca or Anna are around and Gus and Rachel don't mind keeping an eye out for you, we're going to let you go down to surf on your own."

Mum nibbles her lip. She twists her hands in her lap. She sends me this big brave smile. "But you have to promise that you'll never go in alone, Maya," she says, "because that would be dangerous. I'd never forgive myself."

I never thought this would happen, not in a million years. And you'd think I'd be squealing all over the place and leaping up and down for joy. But I don't squeal. I don't leap. I suddenly feel quiet and serious, like the hush of a cathedral or a temple is moving inside me. I twist my fingers round and round. I hunt in my brain for a wonderful word to thank them, a beautiful one, like a yellow butterfly. But my throat is full of lumps that I can't swallow down. My eyes are full of tears.

I hold my arms out wide and we have this great

big family hug and a feeling of relief flows through me like a waterfall.

"It's the best thing ever," I eventually whisper. "Thank you."

The next morning I get up really, really early, scoff some breakfast and get ready to go and meet Luca. I'm still in shock. I can't believe my mum is allowing this.

"Don't go," says Cat, pulling Peaches Paradise up on her lap when I head for the door. "Stay at home with me. We could make a merman or another mobile or watch a film."

"I thought I wasn't any fun to play with," I say. "I thought Chloe was much better than me."

"Well… she is…" she says. "It's just I don't like you going in the sea."

"I've told you before, Cat," I snap, "you can't control me. I'm allowed out."

The surf is zabaloosh and I rip. Luca's watching me, clapping and whistling, and I feel freer and wilder than the freest girl alive. And even when this kook drops in on me and wipes me out I really don't care. There's the sun and the surf and I'm allowed out alone and Mum and Dad and Cat and her spiteful words have disappeared. I'm so stoked, nothing else matters. It's just me with my arms stretched wide, ripping up the gnarly waves. And it's weird because I know I'm only down on the bay and stuff, and Mum and Dad and Cat can still see me with Dad's binoculars from the house, but somehow I feel a little bit older, even a little bit bigger than twelve.

Cat's getting her rabbit today so she and Chloe will be stuck together with invisible glue. I like Chloe and it's nice that she and Cat are friends and they both have someone to start school with, but I kind of wish I could go back to St Cuthbert's Primary with them. I wish I still had a red jumper and a grey book bag and could sing all the hymns and stuff in assembly. I do like my school, but St Cuthbert's was cosy. The other day, Cat and Chloe were all friendly in the hammock, touching arms.

I saw them looking at books and laughing. I saw Cat's 'Life Story Book' glinting in the sun and the pages were turning and Cat was telling Chloe about everything inside. I went up a bit closer and kind of pretended I was picking flowers for Mum, but then Cat saw me and slammed the book shut and stuffed it to the bottom of the pile.

"It's not for anyone's eyes," she said. "Only special people."

"Do you think you'd like surfing, Chloe?" I ask, when I'm home from the beach and we're sitting on the grass next to the rabbit run. I feel kind of weird, like I'm much, much older than Cat and Chloe, like I'm a teenager already.

"Probably," smiles Chloe, holding out a lettuce leaf for Cat's rabbit. "It might be a bit tricky and I'd need lots of help getting out there, balancing and stuff. And I couldn't stand up or anything; I'd just have to bodyboard. But I love trying new things. Maybe one day I'll even manage to surf."

"Don't you hate it," I say, stroking Peaches

Paradise so she's not too jealous of the rabbit, "you know, not being able to do what you want? Not being able to run around and be totally wild and free?"

"Sometimes," she sighs, "but it depends. My dad says we're wild and free already, but most people don't know it. They think their body is who they really are. But it's not true; we're much more than just our bodies."

"Does your dad believe we chose our lives and our parents and everything before we're born?" I say. "When we're just tiny stars in the sky? Mine does."

Chloe shakes her head and laughs like she's watching a secret memory. She fiddles with the metal splint on her leg. "I don't know. Dad says our minds get us twisted up in knots because we have trouble accepting reality. Like if I just kept going on and on about wanting to run around like you when it's never going to happen. I just have to get used to the body I have."

Chloe's got me thinking and I wish I could be happy with things the way they are, I wish I could be pleased that I'm allowed surfing and not go on and on about wanting more. But it's really hard when Luca's allowed to go wherever he wants. He's only twelve like me and he went to Penzance on the bus on his own.

"Muuuum," I say, when we're eating dinner in the garden. "Can I go to town on the bus? I need to get a new pencil case for school."

"The bus?" says Mum. "Why on earth would you want to go on the bus, Maya? Dad or me will whizz you in. It's no trouble. We have to get new school uniforms for you both and bits and bobs before term starts, anyway. We can all go together. I know! We'll go to Falmouth and look at the art exhibition at the same time."

"But I really want to go on the bus," I say. "On my own. Luca went to Penzance."

Mum laughs, as if the idea were impossible. As if I were a toddler, asking if I could drive the car. I cringe up small inside. Cat sniggers and nibbles

and slides closer to Chloe. Mum shakes her head; she grips the edge of the table and glances over and Alfie's shrub number five, a beautiful yellow rose that's nodding in the breeze. She turns her face to the shade and squints her worried eyes. Lemon cakes and screeching buses and scared flip-flops slapping and deep red petals like blobs of blood on the path flash across her face like a film.

"I don't think so, lovely," she says, her fork trembling as she lifts it to her lips. "Be happy that you're allowed to go down and surf and don't push it. I don't want you going to town alone on a bus just yet. OK?"

"I'll take her for you, if you like," says Cat, stabbing a tomato. "I've been on the bus a million times before on my own. I used take my brother on too. It's easy."

"I'll come," says Chloe. "I've never been on a bus on my own."

Mum puts her cutlery down and meets Cat and me with steely grey eyes.

"No one is going on the bus," Mum says, "and

that's the end of it."

I glare at Cat. I hate her for saying she'd take me. And I should leave it there, I know I should. I should start talking about something else or just zip my lip and eat. But I can't.

"Well, d'you think we'll ever go on holiday again?" I ask.

"I'm sure we will," Mum says. "Now let's just leave it, shall we?"

She starts clearing the plates, fast, clattering them together, dropping a fork on the ground.

"OK," I say. "But d'you think we would have stopped travelling if Alfie hadn't died, or if I hadn't had the accident with the bus? I sometimes wonder if we'd actually still be living in England if you hadn't got so scared." I turn to Dad, "Don't you miss writing about travel stuff, Dad? Don't you miss having adventures?"

Mum slams the plates on the table and holds her head, which means she has a migraine coming on. But I don't care. I need to know.

"Don't you miss it, Dad?" I say. "Being somewhere

different and the people and writing articles and books about it all?"

Dad stares at the evening sun and I wonder if he's remembering the faraway lands we used to visit – places full of foreign smells and interesting faces and hustle and bustle. As if one kiss from the sun's rays will magically fly cameras and notebooks and pens with indigo ink into his hands.

"Cornwall's lovely, Maya," he says, with a short cough, pouring himself a second glass of wine. "It's a lovely place for you and Cat to grow up. It's good for children to have a home and a sense of belonging, a place to build memories. It's good for us all."

But I don't believe my dad. He's not telling the truth because his voice is thin and tinny, like it's a thousand miles away from his heart.

Chapter 17

We didn't get rid of him, Cat...

A few days later, Cat and I have to tidy up the sitting room for Mum because her migraine's really bad. I've been out surfing with Luca loads of times now and I want to hurry so I can go and meet him again. But Cat's being really annoying. She wants to do it really, really neatly, just like her colouring in.

"I don't want you to go surfing, anyway," she says. "I hate it when you go."

"I wish you'd come with me," I say. "We could even get Chloe down there too. She'd love surfing."

It's the same discussion every day and neither of us will budge.

We polish all the furniture so the room smells waxy and clean. Then we puff up the cushions on the sofas and arrange the colourful silk ones from India in pairs. Then we start playing this mad game, pretending we're on a TV advert. We keep smiling at the camera, saying, "Beeswax fresh, it's gotta be the best!" We laugh so much I think we're going to crack in half with giggling, and for a teeny-weeny moment we get so close I think we might even touch. I hold my breath, waiting to feel her hand on my bare arm. But, just as she's about to touch me, she pulls away. She makes a cough like Tania and hops over to Alfie's mossy shelf.

"What's this for?" she says. "I keep looking at it, but I can't work it out. Is it like the nature table at school?" She picks up the little photo of Alfie. "Is that you when you were a baby?"

"No," I say, "its Alfie."

"You all keep talking about Alfie," she says, "but who is he?"

"My brother," I say. "The one I told you about

that day I stopped you screaming and scratching Dad."

She peers at the picture; she picks up a tiny blue speckled egg and a beautiful pale pink shell. She turns Alfie's footprint thingy around and around in her hand.

"I don't understand…" she says.

"There's nothing to understand, Cat. It's just Alfie."

"But why did you have to get rid of him?" she says. "Why didn't they take you away as well? Why just him?"

"We didn't get rid of him, Cat," I laugh. "You don't get rid of babies! He died. I wanted to tell you about him in the book about our family. But Mum said it would complicate things."

"Oh!" she says, nibble-nibble-nibbling on a nail and twisting her hair round her finger until it's all red and shiny with blood. "They took me away, and my brother."

All the sadness in the world washes over her face and a million people sit in her eyes and cry. It's so

hard living with Cat. There are so many eggshells around her and it's tricky not to keep treading on them. Cat's lip trembles. My cheeks start burning. She's trying so hard to keep her lip still and her face in place, but I can tell she's really upset. She starts dusting the shelf carefully, picking up the precious bits one by one. She keeps nibble-nibble-nibbling on her nail.

"That's a really sad story," she says, stroking Alfie's face. "Really, really sad."

"Not as sad as yours," I whisper, staring at the carpet.

Because I'd be the saddest girl in the world if I had to lose my family and pack my whole entire life in a bag and go and live with strangers. But then again if no one's taking care of you being adopted might be better. And if only Cat would come surfing with me she might even have some fun.

Cat shrugs, like she's tired of thinking about it all. I stand there, twisting the duster in my hand, not knowing what to say. Cat kisses Alfie's tiny little face and that feels really weird. Like she'll kiss

him, but she won't even touch me. She holds the photo up to her eyes, peering right into Alfie, like the picture will help to make sense of everything.

"His little face reminds me of…"

But then her voice trails off like a steam train leaving tiny puffs of smoke behind. She dumps Alfie back on the shelf, slumps down on the sofa and hugs her favourite pink cushion. She stares off into space. The damselflies start whirring. Saying the wrong thing now would be like treading on one of Alfie's blue eggshells. And I know I should just leave it, but I can't. I can't seem to leave anything at the moment and I know it's getting me into trouble but I have to know stuff. I want to peep inside her 'Life Story Book' and find out everything.

"Does Alfie remind you of your brother, Jordan?" I whisper.

Cat freezes. Her emerald eyes narrow to slits.

"It's OK to talk about Jordan," I say, "and your mum. No one will mind. I'd really like to know all about them and have a look at that 'Life Story Book' thingy you keep carrying around."

"Well, you can't," she says, sticking her nose in the air, plumping up the cushions for the second time and putting them back in pairs. "I don't want to talk about Jordan or my mum. They're private and my book's private too. I already told you, it's special. Not for just anyone's eyes."

I can't help it now. I'm so angry and confused. Cat's not being fair. I was trying to get closer to her, trying to understand, trying to help. Five minutes ago we were laughing together and I thought we were getting on. Now she's made me feel small and stupid again and I don't even care about her stupid book. I don't even want to see it. I'm not that interested, anyway; it's probably full of boring stuff.

"Well I'm not telling you anything, either," I say. "Nothing more about Alfie, not ever! I have other secrets too! Big ones!"

"I don't want to know anything about you," Cat snaps. "I'm not interested. I don't care about you or your life. And it's not private one bit. You're all over the walls, Maya. You're part of this house. You're everywhere. Dad's even made plates and stuff with

a surfer girl on, with the same colour hair as you. He probably has videos of you surfing on YouTube for the whole world to see." Her eyes bore into my skin like hot marshmallows from the fire. "There's nothing private or secret anywhere in this house, Maya. And your brother's not private either. Look, he's up there on the shelf for anyone to see."

"Shut up!" I say. "You can't talk to me like that. I'm older than you!"

Cat laughs in my face.

"You might be older than me, Maya," she hisses, "in years. But I know more about everything than you do. You haven't even been on a bus on your own. You can't even fry without a grown-up."

Now I'm stinging. Cat's cold, empty eyes are staring at me, as if I'm an X-ray in the hospital and she can see right through to the soft bit in my bones.

"You don't have any secrets," she says, with her twisted smile. "You're too scared to have secrets, Maya. Scared of getting caught and told off by your mummy. There's nothing private about your life.

You're splashed and painted everywhere."

"I do have a secret," I say. "I do!"

Cat laughs again. She goes back to Alfie's shelf. She starts fiddling with the things like she owns them. I want to swipe her hand away. I want to wrap Alfie up in tissue paper and put him in a box and surround him with a bubble of light and loads of angel bodyguards and tuck him somewhere private and out of view so he's not just for anyone's eyes.

I hate Cat. I'm really angry that she's right. I am splashed all over the walls. Dad's plates and stuff with me surfing on them sell all over the place, even in the department store in London! And there are loads of videos of me surfing on YouTube. Loads of them. The only stupid secret I have is going down to the beach that night with Anna. And I bet Cat has millions of secrets hiding under her ribs, tucked away somewhere in the bottom of her heart.

"Have either of you seen the big carrot cake that was in the cupboard?" Mum says, wandering in with a cold flannel on her head. "My head's feeling a bit better and I really fancy a piece with a cup of tea."

I haven't seen the cake. I haven't touched the cake, but I bet I know who has. Cat's face closes. Guilt melts over her skin. And if I had X-ray eyes that could see right inside her, I'd see her cake-stealing secret running for cover, hiding somewhere under her tongue, sitting there feeling like silver.

I stare at Cat. Then at Mum. And I so, so want to tell.

"Don't look at me!" Cat shouts. "I haven't seen the cake! I don't even know what you're on about!"

Mum strokes Cat's hair and tells her to calm down. Cat tugs away and shrugs her off. Dad comes in and says not to worry about it because cakes aren't that important and if the Borrowers have taken it away then we can always zip down the café and buy more. Cat starts nibbling and I know she's lying. I know she's scoffed it all, just like the cheesy bread and the chocolate cake and Dad's special biscuits. It's written all over her face in neon lights, brighter than Chloe's orange wheelchair. I wish I were brave enough to tell. I wish I could twist things round like Cat does for once and feel

big and tall and powerful.

"You think I'm lying!" she roars. "You all do! Little thief, little thief – that's what you're thinking. You all hate me! Why don't you just send me back to Tania's? I know you really want to!"

Dad sighs.

"Now stop this, Cat," he says. "You're going to get yourself wound up about it and into a right old drama again. It's just not necessary. Drop it. Forget about the cake. It's not important."

Cat picks up the pink cushion, throws it across the room and starts heading for the door. Mum holds her poorly head and sighs. Cat's huffing and puffing. She kicks a lamp over, drags a pile of books off the shelf and watches them tumble to the floor.

"I never wanted to come here in the first place!" she screams. "I lied about it! And I never wanted a dad. Or a sister! Not ever!" She glares at Mum. "And I never, never, never, ever wanted a mum. I have one of my own and she's much, much better than you!"

"Cat," says Mum, patiently, "sweetheart, tell us

what's going on. Talk to us."

"Nothing's going on," Cat spits. "I haven't seen your stupid cake and you can't stop me doing anything! You're not my mum!"

"That's where you're wrong," says Mum, squinting her eyes from the migraine pain. "You're a part of this family now, Cat. I can stop you. It's my job, my responsibility to teach you how to resolve things, and I promise you that running away won't help."

Cat darts around Mum, trying to escape from the room, but Mum grabs hold of her arm and, while Cat flaps about like a moth on a light bulb, Mum grows tree roots, deep and strong. I've never seen her stand so firm before. Dragon's flames crackle and burn between them; hot specks of hatred spark from Cat's eyes. But Mum's like an ancient chestnut tree not bending in Cat's tornado.

"I'm not listening to you," Cat spits at Mum. "You can't make me do anything. You can't pin me down and keep me in, like you do Maya. I can call social services. And I'm never, never, never going

to call you 'Mum'. Not in a million years! You're a rubbish mum, much more rubbish than mine. We all managed just fine without you."

Cat tugs away from Mum and runs for the door.

Mum slumps down on the sofa, rumpling up the cushions. I'm jangling like a bucket full of spoons. I look at Cat hovering in the doorway – not quite staying; not quite running – so small and angry and alone.

I have to do something quickly to stop her running away. However mean she is, she is my sister. And Mum has her migraine and I need to calm it all down. I have to do something to help. I open my mouth and watch my words pirouette towards the sky.

"I did it," I whisper, my voice growing stronger with each word. "It was me! I was hungry and I ate up all the cake in the night."

Chapter 18

Mental-o-sea-o-phobia...

I don't know why I bothered to pretend that I'd eaten the cake. Cat didn't thank me one bit for it.

"I did it so you didn't get in trouble," I whisper. Cat glares at me.

"I'm not frightened of them like you," she snaps. "I'm not scared of trouble. I've told you before, I don't care about anything."

Mum got really, really cross with me. She slumped down on the kitchen sofa, picked up her trauma books and started flicking through them, reading and reading, even though her migraine was still really bad. And now it's late and I'm trying

hard to get to sleep, but every time I close my eyes I get nightmares. All the children waiting to be loved on the internet adoption site and the ones on the NSPCC advert keep calling me into this dark, dark tunnel. They're telling me to catch a wave of sadness and surf it for a million years. And Cat's beetle-black custardy hair keeps wafting up my nose. Her screams are grating my skin and it's all raw and bleeding. Now Chloe's there too, struggling across the sand with a smile on her face like her world is made of chocolate.

I can't stop crying and the gnarly waves keep crashing over me. I can't breathe. I'm in the surf competition and Luca is laughing at me and his mouth is so big I surf straight into it. And Anna's down in his tummy with a tattoo of a mermaid on her face. And Alfie has turned into a zabaloosh twinkling little star.

Then Cat walks in front of everything. She's as tall as a house and her eyes are red and her lips are painted green.

"You're splashed all over the walls, Maya," she

snarls, "for everyone to see. You've never had a secret in your life."

Her voice echoes through me. I wake up. It's really dark outside and I'm covered in an icy cold sweat that's shivering my teeth off. I pull on some clothes, grab a towel from the bathroom and creep downstairs. I don't care if it's dangerous. I don't care about anything. I have to have another secret that no one knows about. I need lots of them to prove that I'm not a baby.

Through the kitchen door the moon is a thin silver bowl, heaped to the top full of stars like ripe fruit fireworks exploding into the night. I find Dad's torch, slip on my pumps and creep outside. An owl hoots in the tree. A sly fox shines his eyes on me, two tiny torches piercing the dark. Then he sniffs the air and slips away like a whisper. The deathly bones creak the gate open, but I don't care about them. I don't care if their long white fingers break up through the earth and drag me deep underground.

Down near the Surf Shack Café a thin trail of

smoke rises up to shake hands with the moon. And there's the sound of a ukulele playing music to the stars. I switch off my torch and creep closer and closer, sideways like a crab. This is my special beach, my special time, my special secret and intruders aren't welcome! I hate it that Cat's right. I am scared of getting told off. I'm scared it's Gus or Rachel down by the fire and that they might see me and tell my mum. I should stay away; I know I should. I should run straight back home and snuggle in bed all safe with Peaches Paradise. But the music is drawing me closer – a witch towards a spell.

As I get used to the darkness, I see a pair of eyes watching me – two diamonds, twinkling like stars. And now I feel shy, really shy.

"Hey, Maya," says Luca, when I step out from the shadows into the glow of the fire. He spreads his blanket out. "Take a seat."

I know I'm not crushing on Luca, because Anna is. I've spent loads of time with him lately, surfing. But it feels a bit weird, us here, down on the beach in the middle of the night – alone! And something

makes my heart beat fast.

"I couldn't sleep," I say. "I kept having weird dreams, kind of nightmares about stuff."

"Me too," he says. "I can't stop thinking. I sometimes wish I could switch myself off. Fancy some of my dad's famous pecan pie? It's totally awesome."

I nod because words are clogged and shy in my throat. Luca digs deep in his pocket. He pulls out a long piece of grubby string with a key on the end that glints in the firelight. He opens up the café. It's weird being in the Surf Shack at night. I feel really nervous that someone will catch us and we'll be in big trouble; my mum would go mad. Luca's at home here, though. He pulls the pecan pie from the fridge, cuts two enormous slices, heats them in the microwave and tops them with my favourite whippy cream.

Back outside, we sit on Luca's blanket and eat in silence. We listen to the rush of the surf and the crackle of the fire and the beating of our hearts in our ears.

"Where's your mum?" I ask, when the silence has stretched too long and I've licked my plate clean and wiped my mouth on the back of my hand.

"Trekking in the Alps with my sister." He smiles. "They don't much like the surf; we don't much like mountains."

He picks up his ukulele and plays.

"I don't think my mum likes my dad much any more, either," he says, hiding his face behind his fringe. "I overheard my dad telling Gus and Rachel about it the other day. If they split up, I think my dad and I will stay here, which means I won't get to see my sister. I don't care about Mum right now, but I do care about my little sister; she's cool. I heard my dad crying in his sleep and it freaked me out. That's why I got up."

"I'm sorry," I say. "I've been so obsessed with my problems, I didn't think to ask you about yours."

"S'OK,' he says. "Playing this helps me better than talking." He knocks his ukulele with his knuckle. "Just me and the strings and the music."

"Surfing does the same for me," I say. "I'm like

the wildest and freest girl alive out there. Cat goes practically mental-o-phobic every time she looks at the sea. She likes rabbits and colouring in."

Luca laughs and his diamond eyes shine. His total American cheese accent fills me up with giggles.

"Why did they even put Cat with a family whose house is about to fly off the edge of a cliff, if she's so scared?" he asks. "I mean, your house's gonna fall straight into the sea any day soon."

"It's not that bad!" I say. "It's actually perfectly safe. My granddad was an architect; he designed it so it looked like a seagull about to take flight. That's the whole point of it! Maybe the social workers don't know about Cat's sea-o-phobia."

"It's called thalassophobia," says Luca, "for your information. That's the real name for it."

"I prefer mental-o-sea-o-phobia," I say, "but whatever it's called it's annoying. I hate myself sometimes, though. I mean, I moan on and on about stuff, but I haven't got anything that big in my life to deal with. Not like you and everyone else around me; not like Cat and Chloe. I mean,

imagine what it must be like for them."

"It's all relative," Luca says. "You know, your problems are your problems and sometimes they feel big. You can't trash how you feel because Cat or Chloe or me might be feeling worse." He smiles. "There's always going to be someone in the world worse off than you and there's always going to be someone else better off. It's just how it is."

Then Luca looks at me with a wicked glint in his eyes and, without speaking, goes round the back of the Surf Shack. He grabs a couple of boards with special night reflective stuff on them and some head torches and, before we know it, we're out there paddling in the oily water, surfing in the darkest black. My mum will go total-o-mental-o-phobic if she finds out, but I don't care. I don't care about anything. This is another special secret from Cat.

We catch wave after wave after wave after wave, each one different but perfect. It's really tricky to surf in the dark with the torches and the reflective stuff, but we work on pop-ups and bottom turns and forehand turns. We get better and better, work

harder and harder until our skin is stinging with salt and sand and our mouths are all thirsty and dry.

"It's totally sick out here!" whispers Luca.

Then his eyes melt in the torchlight.

"I really needed this," he says. "Thanks."

"Let's score each other!" I say. "Like our own mini competition."

"OK. But first," laughs Luca, putting on a Dalek's voice, "you-must-tell-me-the-mission-of-a-surfer."

"OK!" I smile, remembering. "A surfer must perform radical, progressive manoeuvres in the critical section of the wave to achieve maximum scoring potential! There, see! I did it!"

"You-are-very-correct!" he says, eyeing a wave. "Or-in-other-words-a-surfer-must…" – he pops up on his board – "…totally rip it out here! Wooooooooooooo hooooooooooooooo!"

Then I'm alone in the black. I think of the old film, *Jaws*, that Dad really shouldn't have let me watch and fear coils round me like a snake, squeezing me tighter and tighter. But then my wave

comes and I throw off the snake and my worries and I catch the best, most zabaloosh wave in the world.

Back shivering by the fire, Luca gives me a 6.5 and two 8.5s and I give him a 6.5, a 7.5 and a 9. We both start yawning and Luca throws sand on our fire.

"I'm around tomorrow," he says, "if you want to train some more?"

And as we walk away from each other he calls, "Peace out, Maya! Peace out!"

I giggle because I've heard some of the bigger boys say it before, and I know it kind of means goodbye, see you later, take care. But I've never actually said it myself and it's chinking on my teeth like silver, dancing on my tongue like gold.

"Peace out, Luca," I giggle. "Peace out!"

I'm freezing now and I'm running home as fast as I can. And I don't notice anything's wrong for a while, but then I see all the lights on in the house. I hear my mum's voice calling. I see the silhouette of my dad clambering down the cliff towards me.

Chapter 19

I crack open...

"What on earth were you doing out there, Maya? At this time of night?" cries Mum, clutching me tight in case I fall off the edge of the planet. "It's three o'clock in the morning!"

"I… errrrmm," I stutter.

I don't know what to say. The damselflies are whirring so much I can't stand up properly. My knees can't hold me any more. The kitchen is kind of spinning and this huge black cloud of wrongness is sitting on top of my head. I didn't mean to upset anyone! They're supposed to be asleep!

My mum's eyes are red raw; silver tears are trailing

down her face. I didn't mean to cause trouble. I just needed an adventure – a secret from Cat.

Dad's making us hot chocolate, but the smell of the warm milk makes me feel sick. I need to lie down. I need them all to go back to bed and leave me alone. Cat's lying on the sofa under a cover, nibbling and nibbling her nails. Her eyes are thin emerald slits; sharp dark jewels, ready to cut me open. Why is she even up? Why is anyone up?

"You've been in the sea!" shrieks Mum, noticing my wet hair. She grabs a towel and starts rubbing my head like crazy. "I don't believe it, Maya!" She looks at Cat then back at me. "The pair of you are as bad as one another. Why do you do this to me? Anything could've happened to you down there, Maya, and we'd never have known. You could have drowned!"

"What were you doing down there, anyway?" says Dad. "That's what I don't understand. Why were you even out of bed in the middle of the night, let alone down on the beach? Mum's right, anything could have happened."

He rubs his eyes and stares at me, waiting for an answer.

"But nothing did happen," I say. "I'm back and I'm OK. And I wasn't doing anything to you Mum. This wasn't even about you. It was about me. I needed to do something on my own."

Mum throws her arms in the air.

"I can't believe you're saying this, Maya!" she shrieks. "You've been out on your own loads lately. We really started to trust you and then you go and do this!"

"Luckily, Cat woke us up," says Dad, stirring the hot chocolates and handing them around. "She had one of her dreams and then she started panicking about you – some dream she'd had. She made us check your room. If it wasn't for Cat, we'd never have known."

I glare at Cat. She twiddles her hair, winding it round and round and round, filling the end of her finger with blood.

"We were going crazy with worry," cries Mum. "We thought you'd been abducted. What were you

even thinking of, going off like that?"

Anger and panic swell inside me. My legs are whirring like mad.

"But nothing did happen, Mum!" I say. "I told you! I'm OK! I'm alive!"

"That's not the point!" shrieks Mum. "You can't just go out like that, Maya. I was worried sick!"

And then I overflow.

"I'm sorry!" I shout. "I'm sorry! I'm sorry! I'm sorry! I'll never go out again! Not in my whole life! OK?"

And then I crack open and tears spill over my cheeks. I feel so bad – like I've committed some terrible crime and the police are going to come and handcuff me, or something. I huddle over and my shoulders shake and shake and shake with crying. It's not fair. Cat gets away with so much.

"Oh, come here, sweetie," says Mum, bursting into tears too and pulling me into her arms. "I'm not angry with you, darling. I was just so worried. We all were. It's so unlike you to do something like this!"

"I said I'm sorry, didn't I?" I shout in her face.

I barge out of the kitchen, slam the door and stomp up the stairs to my room. I throw myself on my bed and bash my pillow as hard as I can with my fists. Peaches Paradise claws my cover. She purrs in my ear. She winds her tail round and round and round.

Why did Cat have to say anything? Why can't she leave me alone? No one shouted at her when she ran off. No one made her feel like a bad person. She got a rabbit – a rabbit and a brand new friend. I just get shouted at. It's nothing to do with her; my life is nothing to do with her. I wish she'd never come to live with us in the first place. I wish she would just go back to Tania's and wait for another family to have her. I look down at the sea of stars twinkling below. It was all so lovely on the beach with Luca and now it's been ruined. And I didn't even do anything wrong! I kept myself safe! I am twelve!

I look out of my window at the dark night sky and I think about Alfie. I wish someone could tell

me if he knew he was going to die. Because if he did, I wonder if he was scared or if he just slipped back to the place where he'd come from before he was born. To a soft gentle place that already felt like home. Did I really choose Cat to be my sister? Did she really choose me? Because, if we did choose each other, I can't see why. There's nothing great about this. Cat can do anything she likes. She could burn the house down and no one would get cross with her. She could run away to the other side of the earth. Why did she have to tell on me? Why did she have to wake them up with her stupid screaming and ruin it all?

After a while, Mum and Dad come into my room.

"Maya," Mum whispers, "are you awake?"

I hold my breath. I keep my eyes shut tight to stop my tears making my pillow wet.

"Hey," says Dad, pulling my duvet up to my ears. "Sleep well, sweetie."

I ball my hands and dig my nails into my flesh until it hurts.

Even though it's the last thing I want to think about, the big-red-bus day floods into my mind. It's imprinted on my brain in huge neon letters.

I was seven and we were still living in London. We'd just had dinner at our favourite place and I came out holding a big red helium balloon because they always give you one there. And that was all. If you were a seagull looking down on my life you would've been quite bored with watching. Everyone was just wandering along as usual. But then the balloon slipped out of my hand and I didn't want to lose it so I started running. My eyes were pinned to it, but it was floating and floating up and up into the sky and I didn't even think about the road. I didn't even think to look for cars. Then Mum's scream shredded the sky into a thousand little pieces. And the big red bus screeched its brakes so loud in my face. And I was a feather away from being as dead as Alfie.

When I go downstairs in the morning, the damselflies are whirring like mad. Mum's sitting

on the kitchen sofa, huddled up with a big mug of coffee and her trauma books. She keeps flicking between them, reading a bit of one and then skipping on to the next, trying to weave a safety blanket out of words that she can wrap around Cat and me. I feel nervous. As if someone might be standing behind the door, waiting with a big silver axe to chop off my head.

"Morning, sweetie," says Dad. He's stirring his coffee and watching the toast, keeping his eyes away from mine.

I don't know what to say. I don't want to talk about last night. The whole thing has burnt right into my skin and I just want to forget about it. There are some things that Cat will never have to talk about, so why should I? I've said 'sorry' and that should be enough.

Peaches Paradise starts winding herself round my legs like crazy, so I feed her some chicken snibbles. I have this huge lump in my throat, like a big slippery fish that I have to keep on swallowing down. Tears are bubbling under my eyelids, but I'm not going

to let them out. Not in front of Cat, anyway. She's sitting on the sofa next to Mum, colouring in. Her legs are drawn up under her. Everyone is holding their breath.

"So…" says Mum, looking up from her books.

And I wish I could just run away and hide.

Chapter 20

A tornado about to whirl...

"That's just how it's going to be from now on," says Mum, placing her book on the arm of the sofa and taking a sip of her coffee. "Well, at least for a while. We trusted you, Maya, and you broke our trust and now you have to face the consequences."

I can't believe my ears. I thought I'd get told off about going out at night and stuff, but I didn't imagine this! I didn't imagine ever getting grounded by my mum. I didn't even think she knew it existed.

"It's not so much a punishment," says Dad, buttering the toast. "We don't want you to see it like that. It's more about creating boundaries, creating a

safer space. It's been a rollercoaster of a few weeks and you both need to calm down before going back to school."

I'm like a seagull in a cage. I don't want safe, stupid boundaries. I want freedom. I hate Mum's stupid trauma books. I look at her little bear on the table and think he feels like a tornado about to whirl.

"But what about the surf competition?" I say. "It's next week. What about that?"

"I'm sorry," says Mum, "that's just how it is for now, Maya. What you did last night, after all the freedom we've given you lately, was dangerous and irresponsible. And if you have to miss the surf competition because of it, so be it. I'm really sorry, and I know it's going to sting, but that's how it is. No arguments. Same for Cat. No going to Chloe's or wandering off. No having Chloe back here. Once we get a sense that you're both a little more trustworthy then we'll revisit the topic of freedom again."

I'm a volcano now with hot red lava shooting

through my veins. Cat's been way more trouble than me over the past few weeks, and now we get the same punishment? It's so not fair. Just because they're grown-ups, they think they can just boss us around. Cat nibbles on a nail until her finger starts to bleed. She spits the little grey splinter on the floor. Mum glares at her. Cat glares back. I glare at Dad. I hate this. It's stupid.

Cat and I have been grounded for one whole week already and it's totally boring. I've read three books already and done loads of weeding in the garden with Dad. Cat's been busy making pots and mermaids and colouring in. She ignores me, mostly. Like, even when we were sitting in the car on the way to Falmouth, she turned her face away and squished herself up near the door. Even when I asked her about the dream she'd had that night when I went out with Luca she wouldn't say one word.

"You didn't need to panic and dream about me and stuff, Cat," I said. "I can look after myself

without you butting your nose in."

I look down at the bay and the beach looks amazing. It's so clean and glassy out there and Anna's coming back from her holiday and I'm stuck here at home. I kind of wish I could turn the clock back. The night out with Luca was fun and everything, but I'd much rather have missed it than be grounded for the rest of my life. I wish I could make Mum change her mind. But the more she reads those stupid trauma and adoption books, the worse it gets.

This lumpy package thingy plops on the doormat addressed to Mum. It's full of tiny doll things wearing really stupid, stripy clothes. They look like miniature shepherds in a school nativity play. Mum calls Cat and me into the kitchen and she's standing there with the dolls in her hand. She sits us down, pours herself a coffee and us some juice, and starts leafing through her books.

"Right," she says, handing a pile of stupid little dolls to me and another pile to Cat. "Just for fun, imagine these are people you know."

Then she goes into this whole big description thingy. So, for instance, I have to imagine one doll is Mum, one is Dad and so on until all the people close to me are here on the table in doll size. Cat has a bigger pile than me because she has her birth family and us and Tania and all the other foster people and kids and Chloe and her social worker and stuff. My pile looks quite tiny compared to hers. I've just got Mum and Dad and Nana and Pops and Alfie and Cat and Anna.

Mum tells us we have to position them on the table where we think everyone should be. I start off with me and have Dad really close by and then Mum next to Dad, and then Anna. I put Nana and Pops close-ish to us all and Alfie right on the edge on his own. I'm a bit worried about him there, but when I try to put him closer it just doesn't feel right. The little doll of Cat is burning the palm of my hand. I can't feel where she should be. I try her out in all sorts of places, close to me and far away, next to Mum or Dad or near to Alfie. If I was brave enough, I'd like to throw her off the table or

stuff her into the bin and pretend she never even existed, but that seems really, really mean. I take a sip of juice and stare at the spaces, then put her somewhere in the middle between Alfie and me. But she looks so lonely on her own with no one to huddle close to. I try her out in other places, but wherever I put her she looks so sad and alone.

I close my eyes and hold my breath and put her next to me. So she's really close but not touching. And it kind of feels right, but I wouldn't mind if the wind blew her off the table by accident.

Cat does the weirdest thing with her dolls. She puts herself right in the middle and then a Jordan doll and a Chloe doll virtually on top of her. She tips a big pile of little dolls on the floor and kicks them away with her foot. Then she sits there for ages staring at the three dolls left in her hand. She nibble-nibble-nibbles on a nail. She twiddles her hair round her finger until it's glowing red like a lollipop. Then she puts Dad and Mum just a tiny little bit away from her, but close enough that, if they stretched out their little dolly arms, they'd

easily be able to catch her if she fell. And then she's left holding me in her fist, so tight I can hardly breathe. The damselflies start whirring in my legs. I feel a little bit sick, just waiting. Mum makes a cough with the hint of a song. She sips her coffee. And I know how Cat feels. She doesn't want me in her life any more than I want her. But we're stuck with each other.

"Nearly done then?" says Mum.

"I'm just thinking," says Cat, nibbling.

I kind of wish she'd put me really close to her. I don't know why, but I do. But then another part of me wants to be far, far, far away. Suddenly her eyes flash bright. She jumps up, finds some scissors and bit of old card and makes a little surfboard shape, just the right size for the doll. She fills a bowl with water, floats the surfboard in it and sits me on the top. Then she rummages in her pocket, finds a mini blue mermaid she made and puts her in the water with me.

"There," she says, nibbling. "Done."

I take a breath and soft warm butterfly wings flip

and flap in my heart.

Cat looks at Mum. Her eyes narrow to thin green slits. "You're mean for not letting her do the surf competition," she says. "Really, really mean. My mum let me do anything I liked. Anything. She wouldn't have been mean and stopped Maya."

Mum sighs; she fiddles with the adoption book.

"I know it feels hard right now," says Mum, "for both of you. But this is how it is and you just have to accept it, I'm afraid. It's non-negotiable."

The phone rings and it's Anna asking if I'm free yet from being grounded. Her and Luca are going surfing. She wants me to go with them too.

"I don't know what to wear, Maya," she squeals. "I don't know what to do! He actually texted me and invited me, for real. And then he said maybe we could get the bus to Penzance to see a film. Can you believe it?"

I can believe it and that's the problem. And now I feel even more like a stupid fat baby because Anna's getting the bus to Penzance as well.

"Pleeeaasssee, let me go!" I beg Mum. "Everyone's

going to think I'm such a baby! This is so not fair; you can't keep me trapped in here like a prisoner forever."

"I'm not trapping you, Maya," Mum snaps. "You put your life in real danger and Cat keeps drifting off to goodness knows where and it needs to stop. We need to come to a place where Dad and I can really trust you both. It's our job to keep you safe. Why don't the pair of you play a nice game or something? Or make some more paper cranes or mermaids. There's plenty to do here."

I don't want to play a game with Cat. Anna doesn't have to stay at home and play with her sister, so why should I? The thought of Anna going to Penzance on the bus with Luca makes the damselflies whir. It fills my tummy with this big green jealous monster that has a thousand arms swirling about inside me. Anna'll go on and on and on about how brilliant surfing was and on and on and on about the bus trip and the cinema for days. And what've I got to talk about? Just stupid reading and weeding and Mum's pathetic little dolls.

Chapter 21

I twiddle my hair round my finger...

Today Mum pulls this stupid, pathetic tiger puppet out of a bag, then starts talking to Cat and me in this baby tiger voice, asking us questions about how we're feeling and stuff. It's so embarrassing! So cringy! I'd like to bite the tiger's head off and eat it – and Mum's. I'd like to stuff her mouth full of strawberries so she stops talking for one minute.

"I hate those books," I say. "They're so stupid. You've gone weird since you got them."

Mum smiles. She prances round the kitchen with the puppet.

"Hello, Cat," she says, nuzzling the puppet in

Cat's face. "Hello, Maya. Tell me, how are you feeling today? How's the little bear feeling?"

Cat cringes and laughs. She punches the stupid tiger on the nose.

"Muuuuuuum," I say, "don't! It's embarrassing!"

"I think he's lovely," says Mum, nuzzling the tiger to her nose. Then she turns the puppet to face us. "Hey! Why don't you both play a lovely game together? That would be fun!"

Cat and I quickly get Connect Four out because anything is better than Mum doing the embarrassing puppet thing. Then Cat shocks me bigger than a bumcake. She grabs my hand. She actually touches me.

"Let's take it up to my room," she says.

No one's ever allowed in Cat's room. Not when she's awake, anyway – only when she's sleeping and screaming. It's weird being in there in the day. Everything's all neat like her colouring in, all perfect, like she's not actually living there yet; like it's a cool, quiet church not a bedroom.

Once we start playing board games it gets a

bit like Christmas when you play and play and you can't stop unless you have to eat or sleep or something. We move from room to room and in and out of the garden playing and playing and playing. We play Connect Four and Operation and Scrabble and Monopoly and Pictionary. Mum and the tiger puppet thing can't stop smiling and if her book on adoption had a mouth, I think that would be smiling as well.

After four days of non-stop board games and about a trillion texts from Anna, saying how zabaloosh surfing is with Luca and how the bus was amazing, another weird thing happens. Cat pulls me up on to her window seat to look down at the beach. The bunting for the surf competition is flapping in the breeze and the whole wide world is down there having fun.

"You don't have to," she whispers.

"Don't have to what?" I say.

"Stay home," she says. "If I were your mum, I'd let you do anything you liked. Anything at all."

I'm about to say that, if she were my mum, she'd

227

be much, much older than ten. But Cat's emerald eyes are twinkling so bright I bite back the words. The whole room is full of this little seed sprouting in Cat's mind. I can feel it growing and growing, stretching its stem until it's tall and opening wide.

"I mean," says Cat, twiddling her hair round her finger, "you could just…"

She nods at the bay.

"Go down there and see Anna or something," she says. "Or go to the café. No one would even notice. They'd think we were stuffed up in here playing games. It's not like you'd go surfing or anything, is it? That would be far too risky. But you could just go and see your friends."

A million police people jump up and down in my head and scream, "Don't do this, Maya; your mum will go crazy. You'll only make things worse – then you'll be grounded forever!" But I push them far away. I nibble on a nail and spit the thin grey sliver on the floor. A balloon of worry blows up in my chest, so big it's hard to breathe. I really want to go down there, even for just a few minutes. But

how can I trust that Cat won't tell?

Like she can read my mind she says, "It's OK; you didn't tell about the cake. I won't tell about this."

"But that night," I say, "when I was out and you had that dream and woke Mum up…"

Cat swallows. "I'm sorry. I couldn't help it. I was half asleep and I had all these scary thoughts about you. I got really worried."

I twiddle my hair round my finger. I can't go. It's too risky.

Cat narrows her eyes to slits, her voice is pure ice. "I'm going to Chloe's, anyway," she says, "even if you're to scared to go out. I'm not hanging round here any longer. Games are OK, but I'm bored now."

Cat's words from before dance on my tongue like silver.

I do what I want. No one tells me.

And my heart starts thudding. I feel really, really hot inside, like my head might actually boil over. My throat feels burny; my eyes are swimmy and strange.

"You're so scared of them," she says. "It's written all over you."

"Am not!"

"Are!"

I grab the screaming police people, stuff them in a box and nail the lid shut. I'm not going to listen to them. I'm not. They start pounding and pounding to get out, bashing my skull with a thousand metal hammers, squeezing the back of my neck so tight.

"Come on," says Cat, jumping up and grabbing my hand.

We go downstairs and make this huge big tray of food. But I'm not hungry, just the look of it makes me feel really, really sick. Cat pops crisps in her mouth. She scoffs a cheese string. She tries to tempt me with a strawberry. Then we find Dad in the pottery. He's up to his neck glazing loads of mugs and stuff. It's his new collection, all painted with pictures of a girl with beetle-black hair.

"We're going to have a games tournament," says Cat, smiling at him. She hands him a sandwich from our tray. "We'll probably be playing for hours."

"Lovely idea," Dad says. He puts his hand on my forehead. "You OK, poppet? You look a bit tired, a bit flushed."

"I'm fine," I lie, pulling away.

My head's feeling really odd now, like it's much bigger than it actually is. And my neck's really achy and stiff. I take a deep breath and try to calm down. I'm just nervous, that's all, because – Cat's right – I am really scared.

We hunt Mum out in her studio. She's busy with this unexpected mermaid order for a wedding that she couldn't turn down. Cat sits really close to her and smiles. She hands her a sandwich – tuna and salad, Mum's favourite.

"Maya and I are really good friends now," she says, swinging her legs backwards and forwards. "It's nice. Like proper sisters. Those books of yours must be good."

Cat's words are like Christmas and summer holidays and birthdays all rolled into one for Mum. And her smile could light up the whole of Cornwall. My hands feel clammy. Sticky sweat's creeping up

231

my back and sprinkles of ice-cold shivers trickle down my spine. I wish we could stop this plan so I could go up to my room and lay my head down on a cool white pillow for a moment. But Cat would laugh at me for being scared and then I'd look like a total dork.

The police are still hammering on the box lid with their fists and this huge flush of heat rises through me like a wave. I wish they'd just stop and leave me alone. I wish Cat would stop. I wish we could just go upstairs and have the tournament. It might even be lots of fun. I've never told lies like this to Mum and Dad before and I don't like it. It feels wrong. Cat makes it look so easy. She looks cuter and sweeter than ever, but her words cut through the air like a knife.

"We're going to have a massive games tournament," Cat says, "and we've got plenty of snacks, so don't worry about us. You get on with the mermaids. We'll be fine," – she looks at me – "won't we, Maya?"

Mum sits back and sighs.

"Awwww, girls, that's lovely! So lovely you're playing together."

Then she looks at me.

"Maya, sweetie, are you OK? You look a bit odd."

"She's fine," says Cat, dragging me out of the room. "It's a hot day, that's all. I'll get her some water. See you later!"

The police have turned into an army. They're marching inside my head, stomping their big hard boots on my brain. And God and Krishna and the Prime Minister and the Queen and the American President are screaming, "No, No! No! No! No! Don't do it!"

But Cat's words are still louder, ringing in my head like beautiful bells: I do what I want. No one tells me.

"You need to learn how to be a bit cooler," says Cat, when we're back outside. "Your face goes all twitchy and panicked. It gives everything away."

We scuttle up the path, treading on Alfie's blood red petals, and then Cat turns left for Chloe's and I turn right for the beach. I really, really hope Mum

and Dad don't notice we're gone.

"I can trust you, can't I?" says Cat.

"I'm not going to tell, am I?"

"I don't mean about telling," she says. "I mean about surfing. Go and see your friends, but don't surf. Promise me?"

"I won't go surfing alone," I say. "I promise. But I will go in for a minute if Anna and Luca are out there. You can't tell me not to, Cat. You're not my mum."

My tummy clenches up tight with worry as I jog along the track and slip and slide down the cliff. I graze my elbow on gravel, but I don't care. The gnarly waves are racing and rolling below me like beautiful white horses to the shore and just being near them will be enough. Just seeing Anna and Luca will be zabaloosh. And then I'll go back home and no one will ever have to know.

Down on the beach the sun's so bright it hurts my eyes. I squint them up really small, shield my face with my hand and peer through the crowd. There are millions of people here, like limpets clinging

to the last few days of the sunshine and summer holidays. I'm glad they'll all be going back home soon – back to the city. And then the beach will be mine again. No kooks dropping in and getting in the way, no picnic litter and dog poo spoiling everything. The sunlight's making me dizzy; I really need some water. I wander along, searching the beach and the surf for Anna and Luca, but I can't find them anywhere. I can't see Gus either, or Rachel, or Luca's dad. Loads of bodyboarders are swishing about in the froth and there are literally hundreds of people lolling in the shallows like beached whales, trying to cool down.

And I search and search, but can't see anyone I know.

The damselflies start fluttering inside, filling me up from my toes to the top of my head, whirring my legs like mad. I'm so, so dizzy. This is a stupid idea of Cat's. We'll only be grounded for a little while longer and then we'll be allowed out again. But if Mum and Dad find out we've disobeyed them, we'll be dead for sure.

I head towards the café and, while I'm walking, I make a pact with myself. If I can't find Anna and Luca, I'll go straight back home, run upstairs and wait for Cat to get back. And I can't help it, but I have to keep on checking over my shoulder in case anyone's watching. I have this crazy idea that I might bump into Mr Firmstone and he'll ask what I'm doing and get really angry and take me back home. If my mum knew that we'd lied to her this badly, she'd go so mad, her migraine would need the emergency services and blue lights flashing and intensive care. My dad would be so sad and disappointed and somehow that would be even worse. Just thinking about them makes my heart flip with panic and my throat feel really dry. But I'm only walking on the beach. I'm only looking for Anna and Luca.

I wouldn't be stupid enough to go in the sea on my own.

I have to really push my way through the crowds to get into the café and, once I'm inside, this hot wall of coffee smell slaps me in the face. I squeeze

past a really fat man, who's asking about a hundred children what they'd like to drink, and through a crowd of laughing teenagers, who make me feel really small and embarrassed, and finally I reach the bar. But I can't see Luca anywhere. I peer through the gap to the kitchen to see if he's washing up or chopping salad and then I hunt around the café.

"Hi, love," says one of the waitresses, balancing plates in her hands, "you OK?"

"Errrrr, yes," I say. "I was just looking for Luca."

"Awwwww, sorry, love," she says. "His dad dragged him off to Wiltshire today to see another one of them crop circle thingies. Luca took his little girlfriend with him too. So sweeeeet! But can you believe they've left me in charge on a day like this? Gotta go! Stuff to do!"

Chapter 22

I go in a little deeper...

I need to go home, but I can't because my legs won't listen to my mind. They're taking me behind the Surf Shack Café to where the stack of boards live that Luca and I used when we went out surfing that night. No one will notice. I'll have the board back before they get home from the crop circles. And I know I'm mad. I know I shouldn't be doing this, but I really, really need to feel the sea. I check around, hoping someone I know is about, someone from surf school, or Issy or Scarlett back from their holidays. I don't mind who it is, but I need to find someone. The sun keeps bouncing off the sea,

flashing bright white light in my eyes, making them feel hard and big like golf balls. And the colours everywhere are too bright. I need some sunglasses. I need to lie down and get a drink. I need the cool, cool water on my skin.

I walk right along the beach, away from the crowd, further round the bay to the quiet bit because my head is spinning. A paddle won't hurt, just to cool down, to stop my head throbbing and my legs whirring and the damselflies fluttering. Then I'll go back home. I tiptoe into the water, checking behind me to make sure Mum's not following, or Dad, or Mr Firmstone, or a policeman, or a judge with a white powdered wig. I look around for God or Buddha or the Virgin Mary because it does feel like someone's big beady eyes are on me, burning a hole in my back. Then the army in my head start shouting again. "Go home, Maya! Go home!"

I want to shout back, "I will go home! In a minute – if you just leave me alone!"

I'm a really good surfer. I'll be OK. I'll just go in quickly to cool down and maybe just practise a few

pop-ups for the competition. I promise. I paddle a little further in. The water sparkles over me, cooling my skin, soothing my hurty head, quietening the hammers and the big black boots inside. It feels delicious. I paddle out a little bit further – not far – and it's really safe, and really quiet. I'm twelve now; I'm OK. I practise a few pop-ups and some bottom turns and then this perfect wave calls me. I know I should leave it, but I can't. I have to catch it. I just can't let it go, not now. And then I'm up with my arms stretched wide like a bird, with me and the salt and the sun and my hurty head cooling down, with me and the damselflies swooping like the seagulls through the sky.

It feels so good to be back in the sea, I can't resist it any more. And suddenly I don't care about Mum and all her stupid worries. I don't care about anything – not even my hurty head or my golf ball eyes. I catch wave after wave, making up for lost time and, at this rate, I could still win the competition. I paddle further and further out and all the silver fishes are below me trying to nibble-nibble-nibble

my toes. And I'm just thinking about going back home when this other zabaloosh wave, even better than the one before, starts coming towards me. Anna and Luca would've died for this one – anyone would. But it's just me here, and it's mine, and I'm up on my board and the whole world and all my worries disappear.

I shout, "Wooooooooohoooooooooo! Bumcake, zabaloosh, big-wave surfer girl! Hawaii here I come!"

And that's when I wobble and slip. I wipe out. I get tossed round and round underwater like a tiny little bit of driftwood. Round and round and round in a washing machine of surf that's filling my ears and pressing into my mouth. I stretch my arms out in front of me and grapple in the dark as my chest squeezes tighter. I need to find a way up for air. But I can't tell which way is up and which way is down. My heart is thumping in my ears. I have to get out of here! I have to get some air because my lungs are starting to burn! The sand's all churned up and lashing me, stinging my skin like crazy. I

want to scream, "Help!" but I can't even open my mouth because the sea will rush in. I want my mum so much.

My lungs are bursting from lack of oxygen. My eyes are bulging with blood. My head is splitting in two and I'm thrashing around with panic. My leash is twisted; it's tugging at my ankle and I try to pull it off – and that's when my surfboard crashes into my head. That's when the world turns black and a beautiful mermaid with silvery blue lips and long yellow hair swims up to me and sings, "A sailor went to sea, sea, to see what he could see, see, see, and all that he could see, see, see was the bottom of the deep blue sea, sea, sea." I wave, sluggishly. She waves back at me and beckons me to follow her. I can't wait to tell Mum; I can't wait to tell Anna and Cat. It's a real live mermaid and her hair is amazing! Slowly, I follow her further and further down, drifting deeper and deeper into the blackness.

And then these bright lights start dazzling my eyes. They're so white, like the whitest ever headlights piercing through a dark night with no

stars and no moon – so white they kind of shimmer me to nothing, like I'm just space and pure freedom and nothing stopping me. And all my panic fades away. It's as if I'm at home on the cosiest of nights, snuggled under a blanket with my mum and my dad, in the safest place in the world. And suddenly Alfie is standing in front of me! What's he doing here? Well, at least I think it's Alfie, only he's not three weeks old any more – he's seven and he's wearing a school uniform with a red jumper and he has a dark grey book bag in his hand. He hands me a towel to dry my hair, and a fish-finger sandwich with a hot chocolate and marshmallows and whippy cream. Zabaloosh perfect – just how I like it.

And then we start lifting up and up and up, flying through the sky and I can see my body still tumbling away below me in the washing machine. But I don't mind one bit. It's much better here, being free; it's really, really fun. I swoop through the sky like a seagull, circling round and round and round, going higher and higher. I'm as light as a feather, as wispy as air, and nothing hurts any more,

nothing's bothering me.

"Hello," says Alfie, smiling and wisping along with me like a cloud. "Granddad's here too; he's just made me a tree house – it's like a seagull that's ready to fly. Come on, come and see, it's brilliant!"

And I'm just about to step across this amazing bridge with Alfie when something hard and strong grabs me. It starts pulling me down and down and down and it's all black again. And I'm clambering up this hill that's even harder than the cliff. And I'm bashing my knees and I'm so tired and my head is so hurty again and my skin is so sore and shivery. Then my face is pushed into the air and I'm thrown down somewhere and it hurts so much and something rolls me over and then I'm sick all down my front.

And I breathe in the biggest gulp of air.

"Maya!" A voice calls me. A cool hand slaps my face. "Maya, wake up!"

I try to make out the face. Is it Alfie? It's blurry and my eyes are so heavy and tired. Then someone starts sobbing and sobbing and sobbing, like all the

sad people in the world are sitting in their eyes and sobbing together like a choir.

"Please, Maya!" the voice is saying. "Please! Please, wake up!"

Then the blackness covers my eyes with velvet and swallows me again.

When I wake up, I'm in a strange room that's the same soft pale green as Tania's faded sofas. A strange sharp smell stings my nose and the army and police are hammering so loud, they're totally smashing my skull. I wish someone would stop them. My eyes are as heavy as pumpkins the size of the moon, like I've been awake since Christmas a thousand years ago. And I think it must be Christmas because I keep feeling boiling hot, like when I sit really, really close to the fire, and then icy, icy cold, like an icicle is dripping on me.

"Maya?" says a voice.

I force my eyelids open, but the light's too bright. It's screaming at my eyes, slashing them with knives.

Cat's face is really close to mine, crowding in so

much it's hard to breathe. "Please, Maya," she sobs. "Please, wake up!"

Then Mum's face and Dad's face swim in front of me too. They look tired and grey and old. Cat's clinging on to my hand, her little palm sweaty in mine. I try to talk, but opening my mouth is so hard because I think a city is resting on my face.

"What happened?" I whisper. "Where am I?"

"Shhhhhh," soothes Mum. "Rest now, my kitten."

I scratch at the needle thing in my arm. It's digging into my flesh, oozing ice-cold liquid into my veins.

"Am I in hospital?" I ask.

"You're poorly, but you'll get better, sweetheart," soothes Dad. "You had an accident in the water and somehow… Cat rescued you."

"But," I slur, closing my eyes and sliding back into the black velvet place behind them, "Cat can't swim."

Chapter 23

Am I going to die...?

I wake up again and I don't know if I've been sleeping for a minute or an hour or a year. It's dark outside and, through the huge window, bright stars are glittering in the sky, piercing my eyes with a trillion pointy pins. I cover them up with my arm and hide in the soft velvet black box. The police are still hammering; their big black boots are still stomping on my skull.

"What's happening to me?" I croak. "My head hurts so much."

Mum holds my hand and strokes it.

"You're poorly, sweetie," she says. "You've been

here for a few days now. Hopefully we can take you home soon. Will you have a drink? Something to eat?"

Dad helps me sit up. I take a tiny sip of water, but I have to keep my eyes closed because it hurts too much to open them. And just sipping the water really tires me out. My body is so heavy, like I'm made of lead.

"What's wrong with me?" I whisper.

"You're going to be OK," says Dad, stroking my head. "You've had some kind of nasty virus – viral meningitis – but we're not certain yet. It must've been coming on before you went surfing, poppet."

"Am I going to die?" I say. "People die from meningitis."

"No, darling, no," says Mum, "but you've been a really poorly girl. We've been so worried about you. But you're not going to die. We're sure of that."

The next time I wake up I hear loads of clattering going on. A man in a green outfit is cleaning the floors with a bucket and mop. It must be morning because a milky sun is peeping into my room and

I wonder how many days of my life I've missed. I open my eyes just a tiny bit to see if it still hurts and it does a bit, but it's more like thumbs pressing into them than pins. The police and the army must be dozing. Mum's snoozing in the chair next to my bed, but as soon as I move she's awake.

"Hello, sweetie," she says, feeling my forehead. "How you feeling?"

"A tiny bit better, I think."

Mum smiles. Her eyes shine. And then the memory of what happened drops on my head like heavy black rock from the cliff. It floods through my body like ice in my veins instead of blood. I don't know what to say, or where to start. My mind feels so cloggy and heavy; my head's still really, really sore. But I need to say something.

I wish I could just turn back the clock and say 'No' to Cat. I wish I'd just stayed home with her and got bored and played games. I wish I hadn't minded about not being allowed out. Maybe if I lie here long enough the whole story will just evaporate. Then we can start again and

pretend it never happened.

"Hey," says Mum, holding my hand, "you look worried. Don't think too hard; we've plenty of time to unravel things. Right now we just need to get you well."

I stay in the hospital for one more day and then they let me go home. Everything feels so different. The surf competition's finished and all the bunting's been taken down. Georgia Timson won the under thirteens, but that doesn't matter now. I'm never going surfing again. Not ever. It's too dangerous. My mum was right; Cat was right.

Mum comes over and puts a cool flannel on my head.

"I saw Alfie," I say, "when I was under the water. He was seven and in St Cuthbert's uniform; he had a grey book bag and everything."

Mum nibbles her lip. Her eyes fill up with tears.

"It was really weird," I say. "Everything went all white and soft and peaceful. I kind of drifted off and I wasn't scared any more. I felt free and

wispy, like nothing mattered, like even being alive didn't matter any more. And then suddenly Alfie was there, calling me to go and play with him in his tree house that Granddad made. It was beautiful, like a bird – like our house, really. Like a seagull ready to fly."

Mum takes hold of my hand and presses it to her lips to kiss. There's so much string to unravel between us, so much stuff to say, it might take forever. A lump as big as a plum swells up in my throat.

"I'm really, really sorry," I say, "for going out without telling you and for surfing on my own. It was a stupid thing to do."

Huge silver tears start rolling down my cheeks.

"I just got really cross about being grounded," I say. "I've tried really hard with Cat and she's done so many things she shouldn't do and I only did one. And I hate it that you're so scared of everything since Alfie and the bus. I'm so sad you don't want adventures any more. You've kind of disappeared and I miss you, Mum. I want you back. I didn't

mean to surf. I tried to find Luca and Anna, but I was just so hot and the water looked cool."

Silver tears roll down Mum's cheeks too. She fiddles with her fingers; she nibbles her lip.

"I was so scared, Maya," she says. Her voice is low and husky, trembly and scared. "When the hospital phoned us, I nearly went crazy. I thought you were safe. If it wasn't for Cat you might... I couldn't have lived through that, Maya. I can't lose you as well!"

"Well, you won't have to worry about me surfing any more," I say. "You're right – it's too dangerous. I quit."

"I'm just so sad," says Mum, twiddling her fingers, "that you lied to me. I don't know how to be with that. I don't know what to say."

I try to swallow, but my throat is blocked with shame.

"I've been so scared of losing you," she says, her voice steadier than I've heard it in ages. "I've been afraid of you growing up and meeting the world and spreading your wings. And I've kept you too

252

close. I can see now that's not been healthy. It's your beautiful life, Maya. I need to let you live it. But how can I trust that you'll tell me the truth after this?"

Dad brings in a tray of soup and bread for me. He looks so sad. He wipes my tears with his hanky. He plants a kiss on my cheek.

"It's so painful, Maya," he says, "knowing that you lied to us. Knowing you might have died because of that."

Cat barges in holding her 'Life Story Book' under her arm.

"It was all my fault," she says. "I told Maya to go. I'm the liar, not her."

Mum and Dad look at me.

But I can't see anything because my eyes are swimming with tears.

Chapter 24

What was it like...?

Cat lifts the soup spoon and carefully feeds me. She tears the bread into tiny bite-sized chunks.

"I'm sorry for making you lie," she whispers, "but you were an idiot. You weren't supposed to surf. I told you! I need to tell you other stuff too. But in a minute, when you've eaten your lunch."

When she's finished feeding me, she puts down the tray and sits close. Not so close that we're touching arms or anything, but close enough that I can smell her hair. Then Cat rests the 'Life Story Book' across our laps and opens the first page. And there she is, a teeny-weeny little baby with a big

fluffy tuft of black hair. And there she is again: a toddler in a pushchair with her mum standing next to her.

"Here's the flat we lived in when I was born," she says. She presses her thumb over the photo and smiles. She points at a window. "That was the bedroom. I don't remember it, though."

We go through page after page of Cat's book. She shows me all the different people she's lived with in all the different foster homes. She shows me photos of the social workers she's had, and some of her schoolteachers in all her different schools.

"What was it like?" I say. "You know, moving around so much?"

Cat shrugs. She nibble-nibble-nibbles on a nail.

"My photos are nothing special," she says, "except to me. They're not like your brilliant ones on the walls."

"I think they're really special, Cat," I say. "Maybe we could put some up on the wall next to mine? If you wanted."

255

She shrugs again. She bites her lip. She turns the page.

"These are the precious-est ones," she says, stroking a little boy's face, smoothing his beetle-black hair, "because they're of Jordan. I'd run through a burning house to rescue these."

She hugs her book to her chest and is so quiet for a moment we'd hear a feather if it dropped to the floor.

"I'll be with him again," she says, "I promise you. I just have to grow up a bit more. I've promised him that one day I'll go and find him and we'll get a really nice flat somewhere and it'll be warm and cosy with a big fridge full of food. And it'll be just me and Jordan forever. Not our stupid mum and her wine and her stupid boyfriends." She looks at me. "Well, maybe you can come over for sleepovers sometimes," she says, "and round to play and stuff. And Chloe can stay, of course."

Cat strokes Jordan for a while, her eyes dull green like pond water. She stares into space and thinks.

"I need to know what happened," I say, "in the

water. I mean, why were you even there, Cat? Why weren't you at Chloe's? I thought you hated the water."

"When I got to Chloe's house," she says, "I had this really weird feeling. Like somehow I knew you were in trouble. So I ran down to the beach and started looking for you. I couldn't find you for ages and ages. And I was just about to run back home and get Mum when I saw you, far, far away from the crowd, tumbling around in the sea. You were churning round and round, and then you disappeared. I thought you were going to drown. So I just charged in. I can swim, Maya, I just don't do it any more. I stopped the last time I lived with my mum."

And then Cat starts telling me another story. Tears well up in her eyes and ghosts from the past cling to her hair like seaweed.

"We were at the beach, really, really late one night," she says, "and Jordan had this bad cough and he really needed to be in bed. And I kept telling her we had to go home, but she wouldn't listen. The social workers had given her one last chance to

sort her herself out and look after us properly. But I knew she wouldn't do it. I knew she'd mess up. She was a bad, bad mum."

She turns back to the page full of photos of Jordan and starts kissing his face.

"Then she had this really stupid idea," she whispers. "She thought it would be fun to go in the water for a late-night dip. I told her it was mad. But she dragged Jordan out of his pushchair and carried him in. She was so drunk, she kept toppling all over the place because she still had her shoes on and she was singing at the top of her voice. Then she slipped and they both went under.

It was so dark, I couldn't see them anywhere; the water was all cloudy and black. So I just charged in. But, once I'd found them, Jordan kept slipping away from me and my mum kept falling down. I kept slipping under. Mum was really heavy. I couldn't choose between them. I couldn't let my brother die! I couldn't leave my mum! So I just clung on and on and I was freezing cold. We all nearly drowned. I just about dragged them to the shore and I hit

Jordan's back to make him cough up all the water in his lungs. Then I had to get them home and put them both to bed so nobody would find out."

I'm totally silent, listening to Cat. I'm holding my breath and not moving one bit. Never in my whole life have I done anything as brave as Cat. I've never had to worry about anyone's cough or put anyone else to bed. A single silver tear runs down her face. She nibbles on a nail. She twiddles her hair round and round and round. She swallows hard. She turns to the page with pictures of her mum and punches her right in the face, over and over and over, until the photos crumple.

"And then she made me swear never to tell anyone," she says, punching again, "because if they found out, she said we'd definitely go back into care. And I didn't want that. I don't care about her, but I'd have done anything to stay with Jordan. He's so sad when I'm not there. He gets all lonely."

I wish I had some precious words for Cat, ones made of silver or gold, or like Nana's special crystal glasses – something to soothe her.

259

"Are you well enough to come up to my room for a minute?" she asks.

She takes my hand and clings on tight while we creep past Mum and Dad, and up the stairs, past the photos of me, past the stripy lighthouse on the wall and the seagull hanging from a spring and our paper-crane mobile.

"I want to show you something," she says, "but I'm a bit scared. I feel a bit shy."

Cat sits me on the carpet in front of her wardrobe and gently opens the door. There, at the bottom, all laid out neatly like an altar in a church are photos of Jordan and tiny hand-print paintings from his old school and seashells and driftwood from the bay. And scattered between the things are dried up bits of biscuit, crumbled up bits of cake and cheesy garlic bread.

My heart swells up to my eyes and makes me cry.

"What's it for?"

"I know it sounds silly," Cat says, picking up a photo and hugging it, "but I'm worried he's not getting enough to eat. I thought if I had food here

for him it would kind of bring him good luck. It might be a way of still caring for him."

Cat starts nibble-nibble-nibbling on a nail; she starts twiddling her hair round and round and round until her finger glows bright red. I really want to hug her and make it better. I want to tell her not to worry. But she'll never stop worrying about Jordan.

"I was wondering…" she says. "You see, I think Jordan gets quite lonely up here on his own, and I was wondering… if maybe you think he could share the shelf with Alfie? If Mum and Dad and you would mind them both being on there together?"

And I'm about to say, "Yes, that's brilliant idea, Cat," when her words ring in my brain like bells.

"You called her 'Mum'!" I say. "I thought you were never going to do that."

"I probably was," Cat says, smiling, "eventually. It just felt a bit weird, a bit like I wouldn't love my own mum any more. And I do hate her and I know she's a really rubbish mum… but she is my mum."

"Do you really hate it here?" I ask. "Do you really hate me?"

Cat shakes her head.

"Not really," she says. "I'm just scared of letting myself love you in case I get taken away again. Then I'd lose you as well as Jordan."

I carefully slide my hand over to hers until our fingertips are touching. She takes a sharp breath in, but doesn't scream.

"No one's ever going to take you away, Cat," I say. "We won't let them. I promise."

Then she does it. She sends me a twinkle, brighter than a star and I catch it and tuck it safe inside my heart. Then together we carefully gather up all of Jordan's things, take them downstairs and arrange them neatly on the shelf next to Alfie's. Dad lights a candle. Mum gets some special strawberry cake. We all sit there munching and thinking about Alfie and Jordan.

"I know," I say to Cat, "every time you visit Jordan you could take a photo of him. Then we can line them all up on the shelf and watch him grow."

Chapter 25

If you fall off a horse...

The day before we go back to school, Mum arranges a picnic for us on the beach. It's a bit quieter down there now because the summer holidays have ended and everyone has trailed back home.

"I won't need my surfboard," I say, "because I'm not going in. I'm going to make sandcastles with Cat, maybe even a sand-mermaid."

But Mum just smiles. She hums an old sea ballad and she's packed so much food we'll be picnicking until Christmas.

Down on the beach, waiting for us, are Anna and Luca, and Luca's dad, and Rachel and Gus.

Luca's trying to smile, but I can tell that something is wrong. "I was right," he says, sliding over to me. "We're staying here for good. But my mum and sister are going back to California. So I'm starting at your school tomorrow. It's going to be weird."

"I'm just beginning to learn that life is weird," I say, "and maybe weird's OK. Maybe that's how it's meant to be."

In the distance, a neon orange wheelchair is coming towards us. Cat starts waving like crazy. When Chloe finally gets to us she leaps up out of her chair, introduces us to her dad and gives us all a big zabaloosh hug.

"I can't wait," she says. "I'm so excited!"

"Calm down, Chloe," I say. "It's only a picnic we're having."

Chloe smiles at Mum. Mum winks. Then, after we've eaten and our food's gone down and we're just lying back in the sun chatting, my mum starts acting really weird. She starts taking all her clothes off and putting on a swimming costume – in front of everyone.

"What are you doing, Mum?" I hiss. "You're so embarrassing!"

"Going surfing, Maya," she says, as if it's a normal thing she does every day, like brushing her teeth. Then she hands me my bikini and Cat hers. "Pop your things on, girls. Come on."

"I'm not surfing any more," I say. "I told you. I quit. It's too dangerous."

Cat's nodding her head, her eyes wide with the ghosts of people drowning. She starts nibbling and trembling.

"I'm staying with Maya," she says, drawing a heart with her finger in the sand.

"Come on," says Chloe, pulling her clothes off to reveal her bikini underneath. "This is brilliant! I'm going surfing! Can you believe it? I never thought this would happen in a million years and I need you both to help me. I won't be able to manage it all on my own."

I shake my head. Cat shakes hers.

"Big-wave surfer girl, stoke me!" smiles Luca, rubbing his eyes.

"I don't care about that any more, Luca," I say, "and I'm really sorry, Chloe, but I'm not going in. Not ever again."

Mum kneels down between me and Cat and gently takes hold of our hands.

"If you fall off a horse," she says, "the only remedy is to get back on. And it's the same with a bike, so Chloe and I figured it must be the same with a surfboard. I've been really messed up, girls, and I'm really sorry. I've not given you enough freedom, Maya, and Cat, I've given you too much. So we need to take things gently from here. We'll give that silly tiger puppet to the charity shop and start afresh. We'll find our own way to trust each other so everyone gets to feel safe and loved and everyone gets the right amount of freedom."

"Let's keep the teddy, though," I say. "He's cute."

Cat laughs. "That tiger is silly," she says.

Then Dad picks her up and turns into the tickle monster and she giggles for England and Mum starts laughing too.

It feels strange being back in the water, but

Mum's right, it's good to get back in. Chloe thinks bodyboarding is the best thing ever and, although Cat's a bit nervous, I can tell she'll get used to it soon.

And I can't actually believe it, but Mum's in the sea with us, swishing around in the waves like a mermaid.

"We're going to have a wonderful life together, girls," she says. "I can feel it in my bones. I really do believe that it's written in the stars."

When I wake up for school the next day, the damselflies start whirring. I like school, but I prefer the holidays and, although I'm allowed to only do half-days for a bit because of being poorly, even half-days feel like a lot. Cat's talking like a train about how great it's going to be having Chloe in her class and stuff. And she doesn't even know that we're really tired because she screamed for three hours in the night and wet the bed twice. But she hasn't screamed in the daytime for ages. She hasn't held her breath or run away. She's not stolen any food.

Mum's books say Cat's progress might be slow, that she might never properly recover because it takes time to mend broken hearts. But I've seen Cat twinkle. And, although her heart's been torn into a million little pieces, it's still completely perfect – it still twinkles through her eyes and shines brighter than the sea of stars outside my bedroom window at night.

"You'd better hurry, Maya," says Dad, coming into the kitchen with an atlas in his hand, "or you're going to miss your bus."

I can't believe my ears.

He slides a bus pass across the kitchen table to me and winks.

"For you," he smiles. "You have to meet Anna and Luca at the crossroads in ten minutes, so you'd better hurry up." Then he opens the atlas on Hawaii and trails his finger around the coastline.

Mum swipes him with a tea towel and laughs. "Let's start with the bus first, shall we?" she smiles.

It's after school, Mum's lighting the barbecue at

home and I'm waiting on the beach for Cat and Anna and Luca. Cat's clambering down the cliff to meet me, waving like mad. We're both still a bit scared of the water, but we're not going to let fear stop us from surfing; we're not going to let it stop us from living.

I hurt inside when I think about all the painful stuff that Cat's been through. But I can't change what's happened, because nothing can do that. If Alfie hadn't died and the big red bus hadn't stopped just in time, I wouldn't be here on the beach waiting for her. We wouldn't be here together. Life would have turned in another way and coloured in different patterns and I might be halfway up a mountain in Peru. But this is how it is now and I need to find a word for Cat that's as precious as silver or gold. Because, although she's mostly really annoying, and she's surrounded by tricky eggshells all the time, and she'll probably never completely stop screaming and stuff, she is my sister.

Cat hurries over and sits down next to me on the sand – close, but not touching, but close enough

for us to smell each other's hair. A million words tangle in my mind. I love you sounds too cheesy. I hate you sounds too harsh. I think, wouldn't it be brilliant if love and hate could hold each other's hands and be OK together because they're both true. They're just how it is.

"I haven't properly said thank you for saving my life," I say. "You were amazing, Cat. I would definitely have drowned without you."

Cat's silent for a minute. She nibble-nibble-nibbles on a nail. She stares out at the glittering sea.

"S'OK," she smiles, twiddling her hair round and round her finger. "Anyone would've done it."

"Oh, come on, baby bumcake," I say, suddenly finding the special words, grabbing her hand without asking and pulling her into the sea. "Let's catch some waves."

Cat giggles; she sends me a twinkle, which lands in my heart like a soft, warm glow. And my special words for her chink on my teeth like silver, they shine like a sea of stars at night.

Acknowledgements

Thank you Daniel for your presence, for your tender heart, for holding my hand as we surf the wild waves of this wonderful life together.

Thank you my beautiful children, Jane, Tim, Sam, Joe & Ben, for showering my life with so much love and joy. I am so proud of you all.

Thank you Tim & Susie for the depth of your love – for witnessing my entire life – for keeping me safe – for seeing me.

Thank you Paul for your constant encouragement and support – for the love that we share – for our children.

Thank you my lovely Dawne, for our precious and courageous sharing of hearts... for our long and enduring friendship... for all that is still to come.

Thank you Rachel, Carole, Clea & Helen for your love and encouragement, for the threads of gold that bind our hearts.

Thank you Susannah and Bliss... for appearing... for blowing in on the breeze.

Thank you Michael and Jules for cosy bed space when I'm in London and for all your love and support.

Thank you Vince, Charlotte, Georgia, Kirra, Harry, Sonny & Robbie for all your help in getting the surfy bits right so that *A Sea of Stars* didn't look like it was written by the complete and utter kook that I am! 'Bumcake' and 'Peace Out' to you all, what an awesome family you are!

...ank you Veronica, Ellie, Anna & Kitty Birch, Veronica Yates Justina Gay for all your support and interest in helping me ...derstand the adoption process and in getting Cat's voice right – you've all been such a valuable and necessary resource – the children in your care are blessed by your presence in their lives.

Thank you Chloe for all your help – always remember how special you are.

Thank you a gazillion times lovely Eve – you have to be the sweetest and most gorgeous agent that ever existed on this planet!

Thank you a gazillion times beautiful Rachel – your talent for offering guidance with a firm hand and the lightest of touch is astonishing – I feel so supported and loved by you. BTW, don't know if anyone's ever told you this before but your radiant smile is pure joy to behold!

Thank you Rose for all your hard work on *A Sea of Stars* whilst it was taking baby steps in the world and thank you Lizzie for cheering it on with such enthusiasm and care all the way to the finishing line.

Thank you Eliz for yet another gorgeous cover design, I love it so, so much!

Thank you everyone else from HarperCollins who's involved in some way or other with my books. I have so much appreciation for all the hard work that you do.

I have such gratitude for all the people I never get to meet – those who plant and cut the sustainable forests, make the paper, print the pages, wrap and pack and drive and stack and sell my books – without you *A Sea of Stars* would be left drifting in my imagination. Thank you for the part that you play in bringing my books into being.

Thank you Adam – you were right – so much richness – so much depth – so much love.

Thank you to the space in which we all appear – in and as this...

Love Love Love to every child who's experienced adoption.

Love Love Love to every courageous mother who has had to let their baby go.

Love Love Love x